Girls

By

William L. Alton

ISBN: 0692268146
ISBN-13: 9780692268148

To Rosie and Denise. The last girls.

Contents

Trapped   1
Sick Daughter   2
Home for the Night   3
Murder and Suicide   5
Moving to a New Place   6
More Wine   7
Laughter   9
She Comes Clean   10
Touch   11
You Went Away   12
Confusion   13
No More Hands   14
Couches and Beds   15
Betrayal   16
The Trouble with Chimes   17
The Poet after Her Head Injury   18
Oblivion   19
Crickets and Wishes   20
Simple Sex   21
Breast Cancer   23
Unsolved Murder   24
Sleep Deprivation   26
A Day in the Life of Trinity   28
Destroyer   29
Gratitude   31
Surprise   32
Hopper   34
Choices   36
End of the Day   38
Childbirth   39
Obligatory Sex   40
Ending a Marriage   41
My Mother's Guilt   42
Camping in the Mountains with My Family   43
The Tattoo   44
L.A. Calling   45
Dying by the Water   46

Lila Goes Through the Day 47
Proposition 48
She Doesn't Cry Anymore 49
Reciprocity 50
Favors 51
A Life without Tears 53
Penny Grieves Her Love 55
After a Date 57
Christening 58
Valentine's Day 59
Final Conversation 61
Taking Good Care of My Wife 62
Living with Fear 63
Fear of Open Spaces 64
Anniversary Trip 66
Weight of Sadness 67
Wednesday Night Service 68
Failure to Make Rent 69
Fun 70
Party 71
Things a Son Can't Ask 72
Heaviness 73
Her Father's Funeral 74
Final Meal 75
The Hooker and Her Son 76
Every Night 77
Storm 78
Rapist 79
Cruel Words 80
Verdict 81
Waiting for Consummation 83
Sincerity 84
Voices 85
She Dies in Clarity 86
The Reliable Stranger 87
Forever and Ever 89
Cruelty 90
Virgin 91
Done 92

She Leaves without Me 93
Looking for My Lover Who Left Last Night 94
The Girl in the Store 95
The Question You Should Never Ask 96
Gardening on Sunday 97
Children 98
Night Routine 99
Fear 100
Casual Sex 101
This is How it Works 102
This Is What It's About 103
Living Alone 104
Death Ruined Everything 106
Split Between Love and Obligation 107
Their First Date 108
Inevitable 109
A New Lover 110
Dinner and Breakfast 111
Breaking Up 112
He Drinks Too Much 113
Comfort 114
Silence 115
Save it for Morning 116
The Girl Finally Arrives 117
Foreplay 118
No Beauty 119
More than a Rumor, Less than a Promise 120
Lily 121
Travels 122
Entanglement 123
A Lucky Man 124
Alone in the World 125
After the Last Miscarriage 126
A Poverty of Touch 127
Audry's Tongue 128
A Young Woman Visits Her Mother 130
A Temporary Patch 131
What to Do with Herself 132
Working on Work 133

What Age Brings Sometimes   134
Someday   135
An Old Man's Day   136

ACKNOWLEDGEMENTS

"An Old Man's Day"	*Burning Word*
"Someday"	*Eunoia*
"What Age Brings Sometimes"	*Eunoia*
"What to do with Herself"	*Eunoia*
"Working on Work"	*Eunoia*
"Children"	*St. Somewhere*
"The Question You Should Never Ask"	*St. Somewhere*
"Final Meal"	*Subliminal Interiors*
"A Day in the Life of Trinity"	*Third Wednesday*
"Simple Sex"	*Third Wednesday*
"Sleep Deprivation"	*Third Wednesday*
"A Temporary Patch"	*Tower*
"Breaking Up"	*Tower*
"Confusion"	*Tower*
"Couches and Beds"	*Tower*
"Dinner and Breakfast"	*Tower*

Girls

,

Trapped

The storm brought wind and rain. It brought tree limbs to the ground and ripples to the water in the wetlands at the edge of town. Wild flowers tossed their petals up and cherry blossoms twisted in the gutters. The storm brought you to my apartment.

We sat together in the living room getting drunk. We smoked cigarettes and talked about depression and loneliness. We ate devilled eggs and brownies I made the day before. You closed your eyes for a second and spilled your beer.

Are you tired? I asked. *A little*, you said. I offered you my bed. My couch was comfortable enough. *You can sleep with me*, you said. I didn't know how to respond. Was this about sex or sleep? I didn't want to get it wrong and ruin a good night. You laughed. *Take a hint,* you said.

We showered before bed and you kissed your way down my body. I held you and smiled. I moaned when you touched me. Flesh pressed against flesh. You never once opened your eyes, letting me lead you to orgasm.

In the morning, the storm had passed over us. We stood on the patio and surveyed the broken branches, the leaves torn free. We walked down the street to your car. You kissed me then and promised to come by after work. You drove away and I wondered who'd watch your kids.

Sick Daughter

A plume of smoke drifts out of the fireplace into the room. Everything smells of pine burning. She sits on the hearth, poking at the fire, opening and shutting the flue. She is warm here. Outside winter struggles with spring for dominion. She makes a mug of cider and takes it out to the patio to smoke a cigarette. Her daughter lies on the couch with a blanket and a book. She's been feverish and sick for days now.

Her daughter rises and makes her way to the bathroom. She starts the shower and lets the hot water soak through her skin to the bones that lie there. After her cigarette, she sticks her head through the doorway. *Going to the store,* she shouts. *Be right back.* But no one's listening and when she's gone, it's as if she evaporated.

At the store, she buys cigarettes and beer. She picks up a steak and potatoes, more soup. She goes home and finds her daughter on the couch again. *Where were you?* her daughter asks. *The store,* she says. *You should've said something.*

She makes soup and brings it to her daughter. Her daughter sits up and sips the broth. She watches her and goes back to the hearth. Her daughter is healing, even in the cold room. Things are beginning to come together. Tomorrow, she'll return to work.

Home for the Night

Every day passes with the unstoppable forward momentum of time. Each day begins, swells and shrivels into night. Jennifer wakes, showers and eats toast before work. She gets in her car and aims it down the street. She drives with caution, watching the rest of the cars, the pedestrians, the houses built like blocks in the city. At work, she does her job and looks forward to stepping out for a cigarette, a chance to get away from the computer and desk she's slave to. When the day ends, she drives home and sits in her kitchen drinking vodka and grapefruit juice. There is no one in her live. She is alone. The men she knows are all too familiar. There's never going to be anything important there.

When the vodka runs out, she walks down to the liquor store and buys another pint. She picks up cigarettes and grapefruit juice and walks home. She stands in the middle of the living room and wonders if there will ever be someone to fill up the silent hours. She needs someone to talk to, but she doesn't know how to meet anyone.

Every once and awhile, she goes down to the bar and sits at a table watching the men. They come in packs and she's no good at cutting one out. She sits and watches and one night a man sits with her. They talk about families and work. They talk about food and cooking. He seems interesting enough. They talk about sex.

Jennifer brings him home for the night. She's nervous and out of sorts. He's smooth and comfortable. They drink the vodka she has and smoke cigarettes in the living room. When he kisses her, she leans into it, hungry and scared. They explore each other's bodies. They lie on the couch, their clothes coming off piece by piece. They make love and lie there for a long moment. *I have to go,* he says. *I thought you were staying the night,* she says. *My wife wouldn't like that.*

She stares at him while he dresses and makes his way through the front door. She locks the door behind him and closes the windows. She stands naked in the living room remembering why she never goes out.

Broken Truce

They fought all night. They screamed their anger all over the street and the street listened like a scared child, huddled down in a corner hoping no one would notice him. They threw things at each other, broke windows, and knocked holes in the walls of their little apartment. No one slept well that night. The cops came and they lectured them and things got quiet for a while, but then it started back up again and the words were mean and sharp. We all said our prayers and someone called the cops again. The cops took him away. They left her there with orders to clean things up.

A few hours sleep is all we got. She went out early, revved the engine of her car in the street, and tore out with a purpose. She took the corner on two wheels and then the neighborhood was quiet. For an hour or more, there was no noise on the street. No one dared say anything for fear of restarting the fight. Then they were back and they came home together. They were already yelling and the yelling echoed up and down the street so that everyone could hear. These two people hated each other with passion reserved only for mismatched lovers. They knew exactly what to say to hurt the other. They screamed and cried and screamed some more. They were on a tear.

No one saw the gun, but we all heard it. It was a crack and a scream. One window blew out. The cops came with lights and guns drawn. They kicked in the door. The bodies were in the living room. She's blown away his ribcage and turned the gun on herself. There were yellow tape and coroner's people. Paramedics and fire trucks littered the street. Everyone gathered around to watch them carry the bodies out, thinking, as a whole, that at least it would be quiet now.

Moving to a New Place

There is nothing here for her. She stands in the living room,
the furniture all moved out, the floor clear of clutter for the
first time in months. She walks through the apartment one
last time touching the walls and whispering her goodbyes.

She drives the truck to her new place and carries the last of
her things through the solid wood door. The windows here
open on the mountains and a stand of flowering cherry trees.
She already misses her old place. She was comfortable there.
She knew what to expect every morning. She knew where
everything was. But this place is cheaper. This place is
closer to work. She can walk to the bus from here. She
doesn't have to drive.

It takes her all weekend to unpack the boxes. She hangs
photos and paintings and makes her bed in the bedroom. She
puts her clothes in the dresser and stands on her patio
smoking a cigarette. Come Monday, she'll go to work, she'll
work all day, and she'll come home to her new place. It's not
home yet though. She'll settle in soon enough, but until then,
her apartment will feel like wearing someone else's skin.

More Wine

She wakes one eye at a time, sprawled naked and sick on the couch. Her body is a collection of aches... Slowly, carefully, she sits up. The room is a wreck. Light swells through the windows, illuminating a thin cloud of dust and cigarette smoke. Wine bottles and glasses with lipstick stains on the rims clutter the coffee table with a mug half-full of cigarette butts and ashes. A man lies on the floor naked but for an afghan thrown over his hips. She doesn't know his name. She doesn't know how he got there. She doesn't know why they're naked.

All she wants right now is a shower. Her skin is gritty with old sweat and smoke. The bathroom is in the bedroom. She doesn't wake the man on the floor. He's a problem for later, when she feels human again. She showers and lets the water run smoothly over her body. She washes away the night's smell and tries to tie together he memories. She went to the bar. She drank wine and played pool. She talked to too many men. She flirted and laughed and the whole night slipped away. She doesn't remember coming home. She doesn't remember having sex. She hopes she doesn't catch anything. This is not like her. The drinking is. She drinks every day, but she doesn't bring men home. She doesn't sleep around.

After the shower, she dresses and stands in the living room with the naked man still sleeping on the floor. She's not sure if she's ready for this. She needs to get him out of her place. She needs to get back to her real life. After a minute to think, she grabs his ankle and shakes. He lifts his head. He looks around. This is the worst morning of his life.

You need to go, she says.

He looks confused.

Your clothes are over there, she says.

7

He looks around and grabs his jeans. He slips into them without getting up. He pulls his shirt on over his head.

Your shoes are by the door, she says.

Can I get a Tylenol? He asks.

She gets a bottle from the kitchen and dry swallows three of them.

Can I call you? He asks.

Please don't, she says.

She closes the door behind him and goes out to her patio. She lights a cigarette and stares at the white sky. She feels like shit. She needs to go to the store for more wine. That's the answer to everything, more wine.

Laughter

Summer turns the desert a thousand shades of brown. The sagebrush is blue green. Dust covers everything. Tar bubbled out of the asphalt on the street. I'm on my way to some place I can't remember.

She approaches me on a bike, wobbling on the street's shoulder. She passes me and I turn to watch her go. I can't help but notice her hips. They're glorious hips. She turns in time to catch me.

What're you looking at?

I stop cold. This is embarrassing. My face burns and I want to run away.

Were you checking out my ass?

No.

Is there something wrong with my ass?

No.

So you were *looking at my ass.*

I stand there stunned. I stand there silent and shy. I don't know what to say. She laughs and wobbles her bike down the street. I can hear her laughing for days.

She Comes Clean

I listen to her walking in the living room. I'm sure she's being careful to walk softly, but her steps creak through the apartment nonetheless. The door to the patio opens. I can smell the smoke from her cigarette. I get up and stand in the doorway waiting for her to come back from the yard. She sees me standing there and ducks her head. *I didn't want to wake you,* she says. *It's okay,* I say. *You coming to bed?*

In bed, she says she has something to tell me. *This sounds ominous,* I say. She rolls toward me and puts a hand on my face. She stares at me for a long time without saying anything. I wait for the words to come, but then I know what's happening. *Is it someone I know?* I ask. She shakes her head. *I met him at work,* she says. *How long?* I ask. She frowns and I move away from her hand. I've been waiting for this. I knew she'd find someone else eventually. It hurts less than I thought it would. *A couple of months,* she says. I nod. *It's over now,* she says. *I love you.* I watch her face and wonder if she's lying. I wonder if this is love, this cheating, this betrayal. *Do you need to leave?* She asks. *Not right now,* I say. *Just go to sleep,* I say. *We'll talk about it in the morning.*

Touch

She looks at him until he lifts his head and smiles. He comes to her and they gather each other in their arms, waiting for the chance to fall to the floor and make love. Her belly is huge now with the baby and sex is awkward, but they make do. They cannot keep their hands off each other.

Sunlight glows in the window. Dust floats in the room, coating the books and shelves gold and gray. She puts on some music and they dance, just the two of them, remembering the night they met, in the club, filled with the smell of beer and cigarettes.

How are you? He asks. She shrugs and smiles. *Awkward,* she says. *My feet are not my own.* He laughs and sits with her on the couch. She puts her head in his lap and closes her eyes. They sleep for an hour like this and wake, his legs numb, her back sore.

They eat burgers for supper. They wash dishes and shower while the sun slips over the lip of the earth. *Is there anything I can do?* He asks. She thinks for a moment. She doesn't want to be a burden. *Hold my hand,* she says

You Went Away

How could I have forgotten you? Your red hair? Your thin
shoulders? I sit in my chair and remember all of the details
of your face. I remember the curl of your hands on my chest.
You were not an easy woman to love, but I loved you
anyway. When I left for a while and came back, you smiled
and I watched your eyes for the lie. Where you glad to see
me, or was it a habit?

I sat with you in the living room smoking pot and leaning
against the couch waiting for your strong words. *I love you,*
you said and I believed every word.

Now you are dead. You took the knife and opened the vein
and bleed out into the bathtub while I was working hard to
make a life for us. I wanted everything for you. I wanted to
make you happy again. Now all I have is this stone with your
name.

Confusion

She loved her husband best when he worked. The skin of his bareback in the sunlight, the muted grunts when he lifted something into the wheelbarrow. She watched him from the porch and worshipped his long muscles. When he stopped for a minute to rest, she watched the sweat on his shoulders dry. He came into the house and got a beer. He came and got many beers. He mowed the lawn and drank and when he could no longer work because the beer'd gone to his head, he showered and dressed in sweats and sat on the couch drinking more. Come suppertime, he sat at the table and picked at his food. He wasn't much of an eater. Nothing she cooked seemed to please him. She tried to make the house comfortable for him, but he was too distracted to notice.

One night, he came home angry. He wouldn't talk, so she didn't know what to do. He drank too many beers and when she said something, he slapped her. Blood swelled in her mouth and she hid in the bathroom until he went to bed. This wasn't the first time he'd taken his hand to her.

In the morning, he touched her bruised face. *I shouldn't have done that,* he says. She shrugs. She has nothing to say. She didn't know if she should run away or into his arms.

No More Hands

Jacqui might wish she were alone, but her lover crowds her with his arms. *Leave me be,* she says, but her lover can't keep his hands off her. She goes outside and smokes a cigarette for a few minutes of peace, but her lover follows and peppers her with questions. *This is a mistake,* she says, but her lover doesn't hear. Jacqui pours a glass of wine and stands in the kitchen. Her lover hovers and picks at her. There is not enough air here, not enough room. She finds her shoes. *I'm going to the store,* she says.

Water sings in the gutter and the leaves dance in the trees. Traffic is light and Jacqui walks with her head ducked against the wind. She needs nothing from the store, but it gets her away from her lover's hands. She buys a bottle of wine and a pack of cigarettes. She stands in the parking lot waiting a moment before going home.

Jacqui's lover meets her at the door. *Don't touch me,* Jacqui says. Her lover looks sad. *I can't do this,* Jacqui says. *I need you to leave.* Her lover frowns. He doesn't move. *Are we breaking up?* He asks. Jacqui looks him in the eye. *For a while,* she says. *I need the room.*

After he's gone, Jacqui sits on the couch and breathes. She breathes and closes her eyes. This is the first time in days she's been alone. The only sound now comes from traffic and rain. Tonight, she'll sleep alone in her big bed. Tonight, she'll stand naked in her room and no one will touch her, no one will try to pry her skin from her bones.

Couches and Beds

She sits in the kitchen and the night rubs the windows like a yellow dog. She sits, smokes, and waits for the world to slow down enough for her to sleep. Midnight is coming on hard and she's afraid of going to bed, because her bed is empty and there is no hope of filling it. She drinks wine, smokes a cigarette, and takes her pills that make her sleep and waits for the dropping feeling before lying down on the empty bed and sleeping until morning.

When the sun rises, she opens her eyes and tries to remember her dreams. The steal away though. There's not even a stain of memory. She gets up, dresses, and goes to her car. She drives to work. She works hard and comes home. She makes a steak in the oven and eats in front of the television watching other people's lives. She forgets to wash her plate and showers and takes her pills. Maybe tonight, she'll sleep without dreams. Maybe tonight, she'll sleep on the couch. The bed is a desert of loneliness. The couch could save her. The couch could cradle her until the dreams start and she wouldn't have so much space to fill.

Betrayal

On the third day of the fight, she gave up. She lay back and let her husband have his wife. She didn't want a baby, but he wanted something to send out into the world. She lay back and when he was finished, she took folic acid to prevent miscarriage.

She gave up having her own life when she married. She loved her husband, but she hated him too. He was a difficult man and used to getting his own way. He didn't believe in compromise. He wanted what he wanted and fought until he got it.

The doctor gave her six more months. She was already swelling and sick all of the time. She didn't want this baby. She hoped she'd love it when it came. She could think of nothing worse than being raised by woman without love.

She found out about his girlfriend by accident. She found a letter in the wash. When she asked him about it, he just stared at her and blushed. How could she have a baby with someone like this? She didn't want to be a single mom.

Her mother drove her to the abortion clinic. She sat in the waiting room and wondered what the other women in the room would say if she asked them how they got here. It didn't matter. The doctor called her back and she dressed in the gown, the latest in a line of humiliations.

Home again: she slept for two days. Her husband came by for more of his things. He didn't bother her, just leaving a note. She slept through his visits and when she woke, she woke alone. She woke alone and there was no one to tell that it would be okay, no one to tell her she'd done the right thing.

16

The Trouble with Chimes

A chime wakes her from her nap. She lies there, unwilling to admit it's time to get up. She has nothing to do, but clean and the cleaning is done. Her husband's picture sits on the nightstand and stares at her as if she's done something wrong. He's been dead two years now and she still hears his voice in the middle of the night when the winds from the mountains sing through the shutters.

A chime wakes her from her nap and she doesn't know where it comes from. It's time to get up, to dress in sensible shoes, and walk through the neighborhood so everyone can see that she's still breathing.

She's met a man at the widow's group. His wife died suddenly three years ago. They sit over coffee and tell stories about their dead spouses. Someday maybe they'll talk about the weather or something less personal. Maybe someday they'll go for a meal together. Maybe they'll fall in love and trade kisses on the street corner.

The chime comes from the church down the street. It rings out the hour. It rings out the dead. She wonders if it's someone she knows. That's the trouble with age, eventually everyone you know dies.

The Poet After Her Head Injury

Imagine a room without windows, a room with only a door, a bed, and a desk for the computer. She wants to write poems, but the world is a great distraction. Trees pull her away from the keyboard to stand under them watching the bark swirl and climb the meaty wood, splitting into branches holding up the sky. A hummingbird perches on the twig and looks for insects in the crevices. She stands there for hours mesmerized. She listens to the crows and the jays calling back and forth in the spring air. She feels the wet drop of rain on her face. She combs it through her hair until it glistens and sparkles.

Imagine a room where all she could do was write. How many poems would she make if she never had to live in the world? What if all she had was imagination? She'd be happier there. But her lover comes and brings her to the kitchen table for a dinner of gumbo and rice. She doesn't want to eat, but she knows the look he'll give her if she skips another meal. She's fading into the fog. She is a bone now, too thin. She doesn't like loud noises or too much movement. It makes her crazy. Her eyes are filtered through glasses that dull the light. Her hands twitch when he turns the knobs on the stove. Little things startle her. She cannot concentrate long, but she does the best she can.

Imagine a room without windows, a room without doors. Imagine a cell where she could go, sit, and write all the things she needs to say before she disappears forever. Imagine the volume of work she'd leave behind if there were only walls to entertain her.

Oblivion

She stands in her apartment staring through a window at the world she no longer recognizes.

Her husband comes and leads her to a chair in the dining room. They eat soup and bread. He asks if she's feeling okay. She has no words for him. She cannot tell him about the terrible pain in her right shoulder, the pain making it impossible to sleep. She cannot tell him that she wants to touch his body at night again, that she misses the lovemaking, the kisses, and the warm pressure of his body while they slept. All of her words have evaporated with the stroke. She has nothing more to say.

After dinner, he bathes her, dresses her in an ugly nightgown, and walks her to the bed. They lie together for a moment before he turns off the light and goes to the cot he's set up along the wall.

She lies in the dark with thoughts to match. She needs to find a way to convince him that he'd be better off without her. A funeral is cheaper than the nurses and the hours they spend massaging her wrecked body. If she could just get outside, she could step off the curb into oblivion.

Crickets and Wishes

Crickets sing the night songs. The streets are empty of everything but streetlamps and the shadows of trees growing in lawns desperately in need of mowing. No one walks here. No one talks. I stand on my balcony thinking of my ex.

She's the mother of my sons. She lives across town in the same apartment we moved into the day we married. My sons turn to her when they need something. They never call me.

My ex and I do not fight. Fighting would just make things difficult and they're hard enough as it is. I stand, think, and look at the picture of the two of us from the wedding. We were so young. Neither of us knew that it would end someday. Neither of us knew that we'd grow apart like trees planted together but pushed by the wind to lean away from one another.

I miss her. I miss the feeling that someone in the world knows me. She was always there when I went to bed. She woke me in the morning with a kiss and a shake. She was gentle with me when my madness made life difficult.

Now I am alone, listening to crickets sing and wishing I could sleep away the memories and wash her from my life all together.

Simple Sex

Two lovers lie in their bed after sex. Sweat leaves them salty
and glistening in the afternoon light. Their clothes are piled
in lumpy piles by the bed. They do not speak or touch or
moan. All of that has passed. They lie together and think
about getting up. They are strangers now that the sex is done.

She rushes to the bathroom and starts the shower. He comes
in and pisses in the toilet. She makes a face, but keeps her
peace. There's no need to start a fight over personal space so
soon after sex. It's something they can talk about later. If
there is a later. There's no telling what's going to happen
now that the sex has passed.

After her shower, she finds him naked on the bed. *Are you
going to get dressed?* She asks. He sits up and opens his
eyes. *I was dreaming,* he says. She stares at him. How dare
he dream in her bed? This was her bed. She saved for
months to buy it and now a stranger's dreaming his
unmannered dreams in it. *Get dressed,* she says. *I'll take you
home.*

The ride is awkward. She doesn't know what to say and she
can tell that she's hurt his feelings. It was supposed to be
simple sex. There was not supposed to be any kind of
connection, but he'd connected to something and she's not
sure what it is. She's not the girl he thinks she is. She has
things to do, a life to live.

Do you want to come up for coffee? He asks. She shakes her
head. *I have an appointment,* she says. He sits there looking
sad. He sits there waiting for her to say something
meaningful. All the words had evaporated. There is nothing
more to say. *See you later,* she says. He nods. *When?* He
asks. *Soon,* she says. *I have your email.*

21

She drives home and strips the bed. She washes the sheets and remakes it. She wants everything about the afternoon to go away. It was a mistake bringing him here. She should've known better. Never share your bed with someone you can't talk to. Never have sex with someone looking to fall in love.

Breast Cancer

The rains moved on overnight. Jamie got off work in the early morning, before the sun rose and noticed the stars for the first time in a month. The moon was nearly full. She lit a cigarette and stood next to her car for a while watching the night sky. She stood there long enough for the sun to come up. The bar down the street was open now. She could stop for a drink. She always stopped for a drink before going home to her empty apartment and the lonely bed. There was no one Jamie's life to keep her company. She worked. She kept house. She slept. No time for meeting people. Not that she was lonely. She had friends from work. She knew the bartenders at the bar. She talked to people at the store, but wanted someone to come home with her. She wanted to fill the walls of the apartment with sex and conversation. It had been two years since her last boyfriend and that ended badly. She didn't have time to coddle someone and he wanted to be coddled.

After a few drinks, she drove home. She smoked cigarettes and sang with the radio. She's sleep for a few hours before going to the doctor. There was a lump in Jamie's left breast. The test results were in. The doctor wanted to talk to her personally.

Jamie sat in the exam room and waited. She wanted a cigarette, but that would be bad. No one smoked in a doctor's office. Jamie waited and read *The New Yorker* while she waited. The doctor came and sat across from her. *It's cancer,* he said. The words went right through Jamie. *We don't know how bad it is,* he said. *But we need more tests. There'll be surgery and chemo. There'll be a fight.* Jamie stared at him. *You're going to cut off my breast?* She asked. *That's probably the best bet,* the doctor said. Jamie stared at him for a second. *How am I supposed to fall in love with one breast?*

23

Unsolved Murder

They found her in the wetlands. A boy hunting frogs with a
pointed stick found her, her clothes shredded, half eaten, her
eyeballs missing, innards spread through the grass.

The cops came with their yellow tape and gloved hands.
They took photos and talked to the boy. The boy was sick
and scared. He was too young for this shit.

The cops gathered everything they could find into plastic
bags. They took samples of the soil and bugs. They made
casts of the footprints in the mud. They did everything they
could.

She was in the news for days. No one knew who she was.
There were a few missing persons reports that nearly fit the
bill, but there was no way to be positive.

She was young, they said. *X-rays and forensic artists will
work on her identity. One thing we know is that it was
murder. Her neck was broken and she was dumped.*

There was a vigil in the park for her. Hundreds of people
showed up and lit candles. The local priest said a few words.
No one knew who could be next. Everyone held their
children close.

They finally found her name. Elise. Elise was a young
mother. She'd been gone a month. Her boyfriend reported it,
but no one could do anything. The cops talked the boyfriend
again.

Elise's daughter was with her grandparents. The father was
in jail. The grandparents would raise the baby. They asked
for a Catholic funeral. The church was packed.

They buried Elise in the slot next to her parents' plots. They raised a stone with her name on it. People laid flowers there and stood and wept. No one wept for Elise when she was alive.

Elise disappeared into the earth. They wrote her name in a log and man from the county brought roses. *She's someone's lover,* he thinks. *She's someone's daughter.*

It doesn't matter though. The roses wilt. Mud pushes through the grass when people come to visit their family. She is a silent observer. She sees everything from her vantage on the edge of the field.

Sleep Deprivation

Sleep has abandoned her. She eats, smokes, and writes, but she does not sleep. She goes to bed and lies there for an hour or more with her eyes closed, but there is no rest. Finally, she gets up, back aching, hands shaking, head filled with the dusty webs of too little sleep. She stands on her balcony and smokes too many cigarettes. She reads the news and early in the morning, she calls the crisis line. *I'm dying,* she says. *I cannot sleep. I cannot close my eyes. I try, but nothing's happening.*

They send a cab for her. She's sitting on the curb with a suitcase and a pillow and waits and the cab comes and drives her across town to the hospital. They take her right in. They bring her to a room and throw questions at her, but she can't answer them all. Language left her days ago. The take her vitals and lead her to a room.

The doctor will see you now, they say.

The doctor is young. He wears a goatee and a tie and a nice pair of jeans. They try to talk about the things that might be keeping her up. They talk of work, of love, of children. She has none of these things. She's alone and cannot sleep. She's dying and there's no one to mourn her. The doctor orders hypnotics and benzos. They should dowse the lights for a night.

The pills are tiny and white and go down too easily. She sits in the common room waiting for the sleepiness to come on. She's waiting for a sign that it's time for bed. Hours pass. The sun disappears and the night closes in. She has nothing to do, but she's not alone. She's in the hospital with other people in the hospital and some of them try to talk to her. She has nothing to say so she listens to them talk about suicide and kids, depression and hallucination. She's sits at her table wanting a cigarette and a few hours sleep.

When they close down the common room, she tries her bed. She lies on the hard plastic mattress with her pillow and the thin blankets pulled up tight around her. She lies there and her body melts away. Her mind makes monsters of the day, but she lives through the dreams and sleeps. She sleeps until early morning when the staff wakes her for vitals. *Today, staff says. You have an MRI.*

She doesn't know what that means, but she's okay. She slept. She dreamed and she slept and now it's time to eat. She dresses and goes out the common room. She can see the sun through the skylight. She eats in the hum of everyone talking at once. Now that she's human again, she can make out their words. Now that she's human again, she can see their faces. Maybe later she'll take a nap.

A Day in the Life of Trinity

The sky's blue pallor fills the summer day with heat and dust. A UPS truck idles on the street with its packages piled neatly on the shelves. Young girls gather at the corner and point at the boys walking down the street. This is a normal morning.

She showers and dresses in the unfortunate uniform. She gets her coffee and muffin and drives to work across town. She parks and lights a cigarette in the parking lot. Ten more minutes before she has to go in.

The shop is cool. Already customers line the walls and fill the tables. She makes their drinks and hands them their change and she smiles. She smiles because it's what she's supposed to do. She doesn't even know their names, but they all come back every day for a cup of coffee and a smile.

Things slow down after an hour or so and she steps out to the alley to smoke. Semi trucks park there unloading pallets of food for the market down the street. She watches the men working in the heat. She wonders if they notice her. Too bad if they do, there's no time to flirt.

She mops the floor and wipes down the counters. He comes in everyday at four, just thirty minutes before she gets off. He orders an iced mocha and wait by the counter for it. *What's your name?* He asks. *Trinity,* she says. *See you tomorrow, Trinity.*

She uses the bathroom before heading home. She lights a cigarette and drives to the store for a roast and potatoes. Too much food for just her, but tomorrow night she's going to ask him over. She's going to bring him everything he needs to fall in love with her.

Destroyer

Night comes heavy to the door. The windows hold the light
and the room is all shadows from the dim lamp. She fires up
a cigarette and sits in her chair waiting for it to be late
enough for bed. She has no one to speak to, no one to share
her life with. She's young though and hasn't the patience to
wait for someone to come with something to offer. She calls
her mother and they talk of Easter. They talk of church,
though she hasn't been to Mass in a year. She's living
through a crisis of faith. Nothing is working out the way she
thought it would. No one told her that growing up is lonely
and hard. She wants to go back to high school where she had
a boyfriend, a boyfriend who didn't see things like fidelity as
important, but she'd take even him if it meant not waking up
alone in the morning.

She was almost married once. She wanted it to last forever,
but then he joined the Army. He needed the money. He was
gone too much and then he died in a crash. She may never
get over that. After the funeral, she moved to the city. She
lived in a second story walk up with a view of the mountains
and the park down the way. She drove to work every
morning and wondered if every word she spoke to a man
could lead to love. She was lonely and she was getting
stupid. She'll talk to anyone.

She walks down to the pub and eats dinner alone. A man sits
by himself. She invites him over. He's old than she is, but
that might be good. Maybe he knows something she doesn't.
They talk of family and work and finally, they talk about
love.

My wife died today, he says. Tears gather in his eyes. She
sits back and shakes her head. This not what she wanted. *She
had a stroke and died on the kitchen floor,* he says. *I can't go
back there.* Part of her wants to offer her couch, but that
wouldn't work either. He might be playing here. *Where are*

you going to go? She asks. *A motel I guess,* he says. *For a couple of days,* he says. *I just can't be there right now.*

She watches him talk and the waitress brings the bill. He pays for her meal too. She doesn't know what to say. *Fall in love,* he says. *It'll destroy you in the end, but the ride is wonderful.*

Gratitude

The woods here are full of jays and ravens calling their names in the trees. She walks along the road with a cigarette and watches the squirrels gathering food. She startles a young buck at the edge of a meadow. They both stand stock still until the buck turns away and disappears in the underbrush. Mountains eat the sky and the stars burn bright. The moon is a sliver of itself, but there is enough light to see the trail back to her cabin. She lights a fire in the hearth and stands there with her back to the warmth. She sits on the floor and opens the letters she's been getting from her husband. She reads each one and tosses it into the fire. *I'm sorry,* he writes. *I've broken it off,* he writes. She burns the letters one by one. She studies at the diamonds in her wedding band and wonders what it'll go for on the market. She drives into town and stops at a pawnshop. *What can I get for this?* She asks. The clerk weighs it and checks the diamonds. *Five hundred,* he says. She takes the money and buys wine and bread. She drives back to her cabin and sits in the dim light grateful finally to be free of the man.

Surprise

Her name comes up in conversation. I'm sitting in the restaurant eating Mongolian beef and talking to a friend. *She loves you,* he says. *She wants to be with you.* I frown at him. *This is not how it's done,* I say. *She shouldn't send her brother to talk her up.* He frowns and eats. He says nothing for a long time. *She'll be here any minute,* he says. *Here?* I ask. *Here. Here?* He ducks his head. *This is the place,* he says.

I eat faster, hoping to get out before she arrives. This kind of thing is awkward at best. Terrible things could happen now. And there she is, walking through the door with her purse in hand. She joins at the table. *Is this okay?* She asks. *Fine,* I say. *Perfectly fine.*

Quiet drops like a stone into sand. No one knows what to say. No one knows where to look.

Glad to see me? She asks. I eat and stare at the table. Her brother takes her hand. *He's just surprised,* he says.

A knot a ties itself tight in the middle of my stomach. This is bad. Very bad.

What're you doing here? I ask.

She frowns. She leans back in her chair and stares at me. *I thought I'd come see you,* she says.

I'm eating, I say.

You can eat and talk, she says.

What do you want to talk about? I ask.

I love you, she says.

I was afraid of that.

Her eyes close. She sits back in her chair and folds her arms. *I told you,* she says to her brother. He watches his fingers spread on the tabletop.

I don't see a future here, I say.

Tears gather in her eyes. I didn't want to do this here. I didn't want to do this at all. I wanted to fade away and she could think of me whatever she needed to think of me.

I'm not hungry, she says. She gathers her purse and stands. *You're an ass,* she says. She leaves and the waiter looks confused. *She has something to tend to,* I say. He brings the bill and I push to my friend. *This is on you,* I say. He stares at me as I leave. I hate it when things like this happen. It plays havoc with my day. Now, all I can think about is the look on her face, the way she left. It worked out though. There was no screaming or throwing things. Breaking up is never easy, but when you can, do it in public.

Hopper

Downstairs, my neighbors keep a dog. A Pomeranian. A yap hound. The dog barks at everything. Cars cannot drive by on the street without setting the thing off. People cannot walk through the parking lot. Late night alarms bother me the most. The barking soaks through the floor into my bedroom, waking, and me driving me out of bed to the balcony to smoke. The dog's name is Hopper. Hopper is a pain in the ass.

Sheri, the neighbor keeps the dog for companionship, but the dog is not house broken. Sheri's constantly picking up shit and scrubbing out piss stains in the carpet. But the dog is her only friend and no one has the guts to tell her to get rid of her.

Sheri talks to the dog as if it were a baby. She talks to the dog as if it might talk back. She carries it through the parking lot to the mailboxes and back, telling it all the secrets of her life. Sheri would be lost without her dog. The rest of us would sleep through the night.

Sometimes Sheri's son lets Hopper out for a run in the courtyard and Sheri goes nuts when it goes into the parking lot. Anything can happen to a small dog in a parking lot. People don't pay close attention to their speed there. They rush through and park and rush out to the street. Hopper could be road kill and there's no telling what Sheri would do if her dog died.

Night comes and Sheri's son is on his patio grilling steaks and Hopper is jumping around his ankles for scraps. The dog is spoiled. Sheri's son feeds the dog bit by bit. Hopper explores the trees and rhododendron bushes in the courtyard. She pisses on everything and Sheri's son follow it around with a shovel and plastic bag to scoop up the shit Hopper leaves behind.

Sheri sleeps a lot. She's on morphine and Dilaudid for pain. She sleeps a lot so the dog has the run of the apartment. She chews things and tears the place apart and Sheri's son fixes everything up. I can't complain too much. Sheri and her son feed me. They bring me a dinner plate, three, four nights a week. Without them, I'd be living on canned vegetables and I can't eat canned vegetables. They make my sick. Most of the time, I can ignore the dog. I can tuned out the yapping. But at night, in bed, when I'm looking for the quiet darkness before dropping off, Hopper grates over me with the round edge of a dull night.

Hopper's bark is gone now. Too many people went to the landlord and the landlord went to Sheri. They put it in simple terms. Quiet the dog or move out. Sheri has no money to move, so she takes the dog to the vet. The vet removed Hopper's bark. Now she sounds like someone who'd lost a lung, but the noise stays in the apartment. I can sleep nights. I feel sorry for Hopper and Sheri, but something had to be done. I don't see an animal as a companion. An animal is a child that never grows up. There is constant care, the constant need to watch everything the animal's doing. I've raised my kids; I don't need another one who won't go away. But people get joy from their animals. People connect to them. Sheri treats Hopper like a doll and talks to her when no one else is listening. It's silly to me, but then, I like being the lonely, quiet guy. No one bothers me. I have no responsibilities. I wake and spend my days doing what I want. If only there were someone to carry me around and talk to me, then I'd be happy. I wouldn't even shit on their carpets.

Choices

Too much heat makes the day miserable. Dust floats in thin clouds, yellow as an old dog, coating the hydrangea leaves next to the church with a layer of grit. Tomorrow, she'll get married, but today there is work to do decorating the parish center for the reception. There are tables to set up and flowers to arrange. There are tablecloths to be draped, centerpieces to be set.

She stops for a second for a cigarette in the parking lot. She stands and sweats and watches the finches play in the trees. Her mother finds her seeking comfort in the shade.

You don't have to do this, her mother says.

Mom.

I'm just saying, her mother says. *You could do better.*

I love him, she says.

Love comes and goes, her mother says. *You can love someone else.*

I don't want to love someone else.

Don't say I didn't warn you, her mother says.

Why don't you go home, Mom, she says. *We don't need you here.*

I can't go home, her mother says.

I don't need you, she says.

Her mother stares at her. Her mother frowns and walks away. She stands and watches her go and wonders why

36

things can't just be right for a day. She goes inside, arranges blue irises in a crystal vase, and kisses her fiancé. She's losing her mother over this. Her fiancé will fill the gap, but it's hard. It's unfair. This is supposed to be perfect. She's supposed to remember these days without grief, but grief finds her anyway. After tomorrow, it'll be too late. It'll be her lover or her mother. She cannot make the choice. She cannot pick between these people.

End of the Day

Drops of water hang quivering in her hair. The rain has stopped for the moment but the sky is still wet and hung low. She runs her fingers through her hair and the water breaks apart and leaves each lock shining and dark.

She walks home from the bus stop and smokes a cigarette in the wind. She unlocks her door and slips into her apartment without anyone noticing. She's home now and she can breathe. It's hard to breathe in public with everyone breathing at once. It spins her head like a ball of light.

Daylight fades and the room fills with shadows. She turns on the lamp and sits with her feet up before going to the kitchen and making soup. She stands over the stove stirring and wondering why she's cooking. She's not hungry. She cooks out of habit.

She takes a shower before bed. She has to rise early in the morning. She has work today. She needs to sleep. When she puts her head on the pillow she makes three wishes and imagines what the world would be like if they came true. Somewhere between thoughts, she sleeps/

Childbirth

Her water breaks while she's washing the car. She stops for a second before going into the house for her husband and a change of clothes. She walks out to the car and her husband rinses the last of the soap off. They drive to the hospital and the contractions are hard and heavy. *Are you okay?* Her husband asks. *Just drive,* she says.

At the hospital she walks a few steps and stops with a contraction. She walks a few more and stops again. Her husband runs ahead to get a wheelchair. He comes back for her and they cross the street and she moans with the pain. It hurts so much that the world has stopped being real. It hurts so much she would do anything to make it stop.

A nurse helps her undress and into the bed with the stirrups. The baby's coming now and there is no doctor. Three nurses gather around her crotch. Her husband kisses her forehead, but he does not say anything. The nurses do all of the talking.

The baby comes and the doctor comes in at the end. The nurses dry the baby and wrap him in a blanket. The doctor delivers the placenta and it's over. She holds her baby and leans back in the bed.

Do you have a name? A nurse asks.

Not yet, she says. *We'll name him tomorrow.*

Obligatory Sex

Come here, she says. *I need you.* She takes my hand, leads
me to the bedroom, and fumbles with my belt. *It's time to
make a baby,* she says. *Get naked.*

She drops her robe and pushes me onto the bed. She rides me
with all the enthusiasm of a cervical exam. We've been
trying to make a baby for three months now and nothing's
caught. Our sex life has become a business venture. I miss
the romance, the connection. Everything's focused on
making this baby and I hate it.

Her face is flat and focused. Her hands prop her up on my
chest. *Hurry up,* she says. *I'm late for work.*

I go as fast as I can, but I'm thinking of other things. I'm
writing a poem in my head and need to get to my computer
before it fades.

It finally happens. I come and she rolls free of me. She
dresses in a skirt and sweater, a shawl over her shoulders.
Same thing tonight, she says. I nod. Hoping it'll be over
soon. I need a break. Making a baby is hard work.

Ending a Marriage

She sleeps next to him, but they do not touch. She dreams of making love, of hands cupping her breasts. She dreams of kisses running down her spine. She dreams of his face, but then it changes and she doesn't recognize him.

She wakes in the dark and lies in bed listening to him breathe. It's been months since he's touched her. It's been months since anyone has touched her. She goes through the day wanting to feel the pressure of fingertips on her face. She dreams of light kisses on her lips.

Getting up is hard. She is tired and heavy, but she's restless and irritable too. She rises out of bed and dresses in the gray dawn light. She dresses and goes to the kitchen for coffee. She sits at the table and writes a note. *Gone to work early,* she writes. *See you at supper.*

After she's gone, her lover wakes and frowns. He was hoping to talk to her today. He has important things to say. It's time she knew about his girlfriend. It's time she knew that he's leaving her. He finds the note and shakes his head. Work always comes first.

All day, he packs his things and moves them to the car. He drives the car across town and unloads it there. His girlfriend meets him there and he smiles. This is the best feeling in the world, but he's scared too. He doesn't know what his wife will say.

Suppertime comes and she comes home. *We need to talk,* he says. They sit at the table and he tells her that he's leaving. He tells her that he's already left. She cries and hits him, but he just turns and goes. She's alone now, stuck in the empty apartment with nothing but recriminations.

My Mother's Guilt

The plates in the kitchen sink were a sign. She washed them when she came over. She picked up the take out containers and bagged them with the paper soda cups, and then hauled them out to the dumpster. She couldn't help herself. She was a habitually tidy person. But this was my apartment and she didn't quite fit in. She came once a week and cleaned, but she never said anything. I usually went to the bar down the street and got drunk. She made me want to drink. She liked having the place to herself. I was only in the way.

By the time I got home, she would be standing on the balcony waiting for me. We'd smoke and she'd give me money for groceries, but I'd spend it on beer and cigarettes. *Do you want to come to dinner?* She'd ask. I turn away. I couldn't go to her house without my father asking me what I was doing with myself. He wanted me to work as he worked. He wanted me to contribute; only I never could. Nothing I did was good enough. *What does being a poet pay?* He'd ask. I'd shrug and pretend to care what he thought.

I took my pills and they made me lightheaded and foggy. I took my pills, lay down on my bed, and closed my eyes. Another week would pass before my mother visited. Another week would pass before her silent guilt would invade my life.

Camping in the Mountains with my Family

Beyond the reach of the eye, mountains rise bristling green with pines and cedars. Oaks and elms tint them yellow and red in September. Georgia and I lie in the loamy earth whispering secrets to each other. The sky takes our white exhalations and lifts them up to join the clouds forming there. Back in camp, our sons build a fire and cook the stew we're having for supper.

We could disappear, she says. *No one would miss us.*

The boys would.

They're grown now. They don't need us around.

I catch a leaf falling from the chestnut tree and study the veins and pulp of the thing. I think about going someplace where no one knew me and it scared the hell out of me. I'm too old to be starting over again. I have everything I need right here.

I love this life, I say.

Georgia rolls onto her side and kisses my cheek.

So predictable, she says.

I know what I like.

I love you anyway.

Back in camp, we eat. The boys talk about school and work and I watch Georgia close for any sign that she might leave without us. I watch her and decide that if she went, I'd go too, even if it meant erasing myself building a new face.

43

The Tattoo

Moths circled the light in the courtyard, courting their deaths from the heat. They didn't seem to notice the zap of their wings burning up or the dry crumble of their bodies gathering in the lamp. Samantha and I stood there watching them die, smoking cigarettes, and holding hands. She pulled me into the shadows and lifted her shirt to show me the newest tattoo around her nipple. The tattoo was a rose, barely opening. Her nipples were small and hard against the ribs running like organ keys across her chest. I kissed her then and she smiled at me. *Like it?* She asked.

We made our way to the car and crawled into the backseat. It was dark here and no one cared what was happening in the backseat of cars. We made out and she gave me head. We made love with her straddling me, half-naked, rushed. When it was over, we got out and went back to the courtyard. Music fell through the windows with the light. People talked and came out to smoke in the night. I wanted to go home with Samantha and show her what I could do in a bed, but she was dancing now. She'd forgotten all about me. She moved through the crowd and touched men's faces. She showed them her tattoo. Once or twice, she took someone out to the car. If I believed in love, I'd sell it to Samantha. She needs something to light the way to morning.

L.A. Calling

She brings food to the diners and takes away their plates
when they've finished. She smiles a thin smile and makes
change for them. They leave their tips on the tables. She
gathers up her money and saves it in a gallon jar on her
dresser. She lives in a studio downtown and rides the bus to
work every evening, saving money for a trip to California.
She's met a boy who lives in L.A. and he's promised her a
life there if she'd just find a way to make it down. She wants
enough money to ride the train, enough money to find a
place to stay, enough money to look for work. She's nearly
there. If tips keep up, she'll have her wad in two weeks.
She'll quit her job and she'll pack her things and head south.
The sun will be brighter there. The ocean will be warmer.
She'll fall in love and she'll be happy. She knows the boy
might not work out, but the city itself is what calls her. She
wants to live someplace without rain. She wants a warm
Christmas and a hot Easter. Maybe she'll finally be happy.
Maybe she'll make something of herself.

Dying by the Water

She died on the beach. I took her there every morning
because she wanted to see the water. I pushed and pulled her
wheelchair through the sand and the sun beat down on us.
The grassy dunes rose over us and the air smelled of fish and
salt. I took her there and we smoked cigarettes in the wind.
Her hair was gone by now. Her breasts sawed off and not
replaced. There was no point. The cancer was in her brain.
She sat in the wheelchair with the blanket wrapped tight
around her and stared out at the tide, as if she could hold the
waves back with her eyes alone.

The morning she died, she had a hard time getting out of
bed. She slept in the car, her chest heaving and shuttering
with each breath and I nearly turned around and stayed
home. On the sand, she opened a thermos of tea and a bottle
of morphine and swallowed the whole thing down. I sat and
watched her until her head fell forward and her chest went
still. I waited a half hour, talking to her about the gulls and
terns. She was gone when I touched her. This was the last of
it. This was where she wanted to go. I wheeled her back to
the car and drove to the hospital. *You didn't try to stop her?*
The nurse asked. *Not until it was too late.*

Lila Goes Through The Day

Empty rooms. Nothing on the walls but mold and peeling paint. The windows swollen shut and the carpet coming up in places. Lila sleeps in a sleeping bag back by the bathroom. No one comes here but her. During the day, she sits on the sidewalk downtown or wanders to the riverfront to panhandle enough money for a pack of cigarettes and a bottle of two-dollar wine. Sometimes, when she gets hungry enough, she pulls a trick on Martin Luther King, Jr. Boulevard. She buys a burger and a beer and eats on the street. She walks all night until the sun is bloody over the mountain. Cops stop her sometimes, trying to take her places she doesn't want to go.

Sundays she goes to Sisters of the Road Café on Sixth and stands in line for a spaghetti dinner. She's usually drunk, but she's quiet and doesn't bother anyone. She sits alone, eats, and sweeps the floor for her meal before taking what's left of her stash and buying a bottle and heading back to her flop.

A preacher man finds her on the street. He gives her a blanket when what she really needs is a cigarette and a drink. He tells her of Jesus and she listens because she was brought up to be polite to preachers and teachers. She listens and when the preacher asks her if she's ready to be saved, she shakes her head. *There's no saving me,* she says. *A bastard shall not pass the gates of heaven.* The preacher tries to reassure her, but she excuses herself and walks away. It's not her fault the world has no room for her. She does the best she can with what she has. She just waits for the day to come when the cold with take her away and no one will miss her.

Proposition

In the club, the music was a wall. It reverberated and bent
with the light from a thousand lamps seat on tables and in
alcoves. The room was dark and smelled of cigarette smoke,
sweat, and ammonia. Bodies pressed against each other in
the darkness. They kissed and ran hands up under shirts,
cupping a breast, or down along the ass of jeans to find a
grip. Yulia and I pressed into the crowd and managed a few
inches between us. She leaned in and whispered. *Do you
want to fuck me?* I closed my eyes. Was this an invitation or
a challenge? I kissed her and she threw her arms around me.
The sweat pooled in our shirts. Her nipples stood braless in
the colored light. I wanted to take her home. I wanted to fold
her in half and drive into her like a piston. I was nervous and
awkward, but the introductions had been made. If all went
well, I'd have someone to sleep with tonight.

She Doesn't Cry Anymore

She says his name as if there were no loss, no heartbreak.
She doesn't cry anymore when she thinks of him. He's been
dead three months now and she's coming to peace. When
she visits his grave, she brings lilies and leaves them on the
stone. She brushes away the loose grass and leaves that have
fallen over the grave. The grass here seems greener than the
grass in her yard. It seems quieter, the trees taller, healthier.
Every week she brings a letter to the grave and leaves it
weighted with a stone. Each week, the letter is gone when
she comes again. They still talk sometimes at night. She
forgets that he's gone and she says his name over and over
again. They say she's moving on, but she's still wrapped up
in his memory. You don't just forget someone you loved for
thirty years. You don't leave behind the greatest hurt of your
life like a pebble dropped in the mud.

Reciprocity

Wind steals the petals from the flowering cherry trees and spreads them over the parking lot. I stand on my balcony and watch them drift over the asphalt. She comes out and wraps her arms around my waist. She rests her head on my shoulder blades. Warm skin touches warm skin and I remember the night, the lovemaking, the simple sleep without waking up once from nightmares. *I've made pancakes,* she says. I finish my cigarette and go to the kitchen table. She stacks my plate high and slides the butter to me. Jelly and syrup rest on the table. I eat and watch her face. She doesn't mind my staring. It used to bother her, but I stare every morning, memorizing the curve of her jaw, the angle of her eyes, the thin line of her lips. Something could happen today to take it all away and I don't want to forget.

After breakfast, we walk through the campus. The trees are full now. Finches and sparrows flit from limb to limb. Squirrels gather food and bury it in the soft dirt around the roots. I wonder where they go at night. It doesn't matter since they always come back with the sun.

I love you, she says. I nod and kiss the top of her head. *Can you say it?* She asks. *Not right now,* I say. *Soon.*

The day marched from morning to evening and we spend it cleaning the apartment. We take out the trash and vacuum. She does laundry and I write poems. Come suppertime, she makes a steak and scalloped potatoes.

The night comes with rain rattling the window screens. We go to bed. She kisses me. Her breast presses into my arm and her nipple brushes my ribs. We make love to the sound of water running in the gutter. She gets up and showers and I wait for her to come back to me. I wait for her warm body and when she lies down again, I kiss her neck. *I love you,* I say. She smiles and presses close. *It's about time.*

Favors

A dog lies on the porch of my grandmother's house. The dog is gray and toothless and just lies there eyeballing newcomers while remembering the days of bark and bite. The dog is the last living remnant of my grandfather. It's pushing twenty years and is waiting patiently to die so my grandmother can move on.

My grandmother feeds the dog, but it doesn't move from that spot on the porch. *Damn thing just won't go,* she says. *I've been waiting a year now. A year since your grandfather died. The dog's just too lazy to die like any decent animal would.*

She sits in the kitchen drinking sweet tea. She lights a cigarette and the smoke rises over her face like a veil. She narrows her eyes and sips the filter like a straw. She's a tiny woman with a tiny head and only a little patience. She loved my grandfather and still wears black through the day. I make us spaghetti and we eat without talking. She does the dishes and sets the dog's bowl on the porch for it to nibble at when it will.

Your grandfather made me promise to take care of the beast, she says. *He wanted me to walk it and take it hunting. I haven't been hunting in ten years. These hands can't hold a gun.*

I go out and sit with the dog in the warm summer air. It rests its snout on my foot. It scrub it's ears. It's time to go. In the morning, I'll come to take the animal to the vet and have it put down. Grandfather would never forgive me, but he's not here and the dog's a burden. Once he's gone, she can sell the house and move into town. She can do things she wants to do. There's a nice retirement community down the street from my place.

Morning comes and I sneak into the yard. I carry the dog to the car and set him in the back. The vet's in town and I drive straight there. *Is there something wrong with him?* The vet asks. *He's too old,* I say. *He needs to rest.*

I'm with him when they give him the shot. He closes his eyes and snorts once and then it's done. I leave him to be cremated.

Where's my dog? Grandmother asks.

I had him put down.

You didn't ask me first?

I was doing you a favor.

I suppose now you'll want me to move to that retirement community.

It's a thought.

Don't do me any more favors.

A Life without Tears

The first clear day in a month, but the park is still wet from the night's rain, but the sky is deep and blue and the clouds are high brushstrokes. The sun is a wheel of light. Shadows make cool pools in the early spring heat.

She stands in the park watching the finches strip the blossoms there. Flowering cherry trees thrust pink and white petals into the air. She watches the world through hazel eyes rimmed red with tears. This is the first day she's been alone in twenty-five years. Her lover came home last night, packed a bag and left. *I'll send for the rest of it later,* he said. She doesn't know what happened. They weren't happy, but they'd been unhappy for so long that it was comfortable. The unhappiness doesn't mean she doesn't love him. But he was done. Something happened yesterday and it pushed him from static displeasure into mobility.

Where are you going? She asked.

You have my cell number if you need me, he said.

There was no fight. Very few words. He packed and left and when he left, she stood in the doorway staring at the walls that no longer hold the smell of him. He's only been gone a day and the apartment has forgotten all about him. Only the pillow smells of his soap. She sleeps with them close, waking in the morning forgetting that he is not waiting for her in the kitchen. He is not coming home for dinner. He will not sleep in the bed with her again. He's gone and she has nothing to win him back.

So she walks in the park, calls in sick to work. She cries, dries her eyes and blows her nose and cries some more. She always thought it would get better. Everything always got better, right? She walks in the park, along the creek running over stones and watches the geese and ducks with their waterproof feathers, swimming in the slow current. She watches the crows rid the nests of smaller birds. She watches the leaves in the trees start to unfold in the sunlight. She walks and walks and walks. There is nowhere to go.

In the afternoon, she buys a pint of vodka and goes home. She drinks straight from the bottle and smokes in the kitchen tapping ashes into the sink. She stares out the windows at the neighbors going through their lives without any awareness of tragedy or grief. It's over now. The least you can do is move on. This apartment is too big. She'll look for something smaller. She'll narrow her life to only doing what she thinks needs doing. She'll move on. Not that she won't look back and wonder sometimes, but she'll do it without tears. She'll do it with a straight back and the knowledge that her life is her own. She'll live the life she always wanted. Maybe she'll even fall in love again

Penny Grieves Her Love

There is grief here and rage the color of a fire burned down
to embers and ash. The wind sings in the trees, squirrels
running from limb to limb. Penny stands at her lover's grave
and says his name. It's been a month since he killed himself.
It was probably an accident, but the pills slowed his heart
and crushed his lungs. He died before anyone could do
anything. She looks at the stone with her lover's name, his
life described in lines and numbers. She lays a bouquet on
the ground. *You're a son-of-a-bitch,* she says. *I miss you.*
Her voice is quiet and she stands in the grass, wet from
morning rain. She wants her lover to rise up and wrap his
arms around her. She wants to see his face when she wakes
in the morning. Their years together weren't easy years.
There were fights and nights in which he slept on the couch,
away from her. But he was always there when she woke.
Now he's gone.

Penny thinks of falling in love again. She thinks of
someone's unfamiliar face breathing on her from the pillow
on that side of the bed. She doesn't want to meet new men.
She doesn't want to go through the slow ritual of breaking
down the walls of someone's life. She stands here thinking
that maybe tomorrow she'll go to a bar and take someone
home for a few hours. She'll send him away after they've
fucked and she'll sleep alone again, restless.

Walking through the cemetery, Penny wonders about the
graves lined up here. There is no one else visiting family.
There is no one else with flowers. She wants to talk to her
lover about the surreal nature of visiting the dead, but he's
gone now and there is no one to share the anger with. There
is no one to understand the time she takes to come out there
in the middle of the day and stand in the clouds' shadows
with nothing to say.

Back in her car, she lights a cigarette and drives to the store on the corner. She buys a bottle of wine and a pack of cigarettes. She drives home, where she gets quietly drunk. *Where have you gone?* She asks. *I cannot follow you.*

When the sun drops into the mountains, Penny goes to bed and waits for sleep to come. Tomorrow, she'll wake and go to work. She'll talk to people she has nothing to say to. She'll smoke in the parking lot, looking for her lover's face in the crowd, knowing the whole time that he will not come.

After a Date

Driving back from the restaurant, we stop at the store for a bottle of wine and a carton of cigarettes. In the car, we smoke and we talk about work. Work is all we ever talk about. Our lives are eaten up by work.

I'm planting sweet peas on Saturday, she says. *Maybe you could till the soil.*

I hate gardening. The flowers growing in the front lot are all her doing. She spends long hours on her knees out there, her hands wrist deep in the soil. She sprays for aphids in the roses and put out slug bait around the lettuce. She grows cherry tomatoes in a box in the back and irises along the front walk.

I need to write ten thousand words this weekend, I say.

Ten thousand?

Ten thousand.

Once home, she opens the wine and pours the dark liquid into clear glass. She sips and sits at the kitchen table going through the mail, all bills, and credit card offers. I smoke a cigarette and try to write. Hours pass and we haven't said anything to each other. Midnight comes and she goes to bed. I write a thousand words about loss. Outside, someone shouts in the street. I take my pills and wait for the soft high that tells me it's time to sleep.

Christening

Come sit next to me, she says. *I need the warmth.*

I sit next to her, thigh to thigh. She kisses my neck and puts her head on my shoulder.

Let's go to bed, she says. *It'll be nice.*

We've only just moved in. Our bed is a mattress on the floor waiting for us to put the frame together. We'll do it tomorrow. Tomorrow is soon enough.

I can't move, I say.

She runs her hand over my chest.
A hot shower, she says. *That'll cure you.*

We get naked and stand in the steaming water. She takes me in her mouth. I buck and twist. We make love and we go to bed. She sleeps with her head on my chest, content now that we've christened the place.

Valentine's Day

My marriage ended on a Sunday. Valentine's Day.

My wife came home from Mass alone. I'd stopped going to church with her because I was going through a crisis of faith, but she still took our sons every Sunday and this Sunday she came home without them.

I knew something was wrong. Her face was flat and her lips thin. She came into the living room and said we needed to talk. I asked if I was in trouble. She said no.
We went to the kitchen and sat at the table and she said she thought it was time for me to move out. I didn't understand at first. *It's time you found your own place,* she said. I nodded and went out for a cigarette.

Looking back now, I can see that it was a long time coming, but when it happened it still took me by surprise. I smoked and she watched me through the sliding glass door and neither of us said anything. When I came back in, I said I thought I wasn't in trouble.

You're not, she said.

This seems like trouble to me.

She offered to pay all the rent and deposits for an apartment. She said I had a week to find a place. I could sleep on the couch until then.

I could've fought her over it, but there was no point to it. She wanted me gone so I would go. We talked about visits and time with the kids. We talked about money and bills. I thought at the time it was temporary, but I knew better. She was gone with me and I would have to find a way to start over again.

After we walked, she went to her parents' and got the boys and the brought them home. We explained the situation to them and they didn't seem surprised or hurt or angry. They just nodded and went on about their business.

The week passed. I found an apartment across town. I moved in and settled down to my new life. It's been two years now and still, on Valentine's Day, I think about what it was like to be a married man.

Final Conversation

She sits with her husband in the little room on the unit with all the rest of the drunks and addicts staying here. They sit in a circle and the counselor talks about the disease of addiction.

This is not something they want, the counselor says, but Amy's not sure she buys it. If her husband didn't want to drink, then he wouldn't drink. He wouldn't drink and everything would be okay. They wouldn't be sitting here listening to this shit about diseases and control. Her husband could control his drinking if he wanted to. But he doesn't control it. He drinks too much and nothing's okay.

Amy says nothing though. She listens and gets angrier and angrier. She keeps her peace and waits to be alone with her husband. Her husband sees what's coming and closes his eyes. He sees what's coming and his belly turns to stone and fire.

He takes her to his room after the meeting and Amy turns on him. She opens her mouth, but nothing comes out. There are no words. She shakes her head to loosen up the anger packed up tight there.

Is this what they're teaching you? She asks.

Her husband shrugs.

This is shit, she says.

Her husband shrugs again.

Say something, she says.

I want a divorce, he says.

Amy closes her mouth. There's nothing left to say.

Taking Good Care of My Wife

The moon climbs up from Mt. Hood. The sky bleeds,
birthing a new day. She sleeps through it all, finally resting
after days of fear and pain. Morphine makes her dreams
vivid and loud. She cannot wake from the nightmares. She
has to ride them through. Late in the morning, she opens her
eyes, but she doesn't move. Her belly is a bowl of light,
burning through her organs, filling her with the dull ache all
the way to the bone. She cannot move and I bring her soup
and toast. She can't keep anything down and she is
becoming a bone stretched out on the mattress. I help her
walk to the bathroom and leave there for privacy's sake. She
calls me in to help her into the shower. She is naked now and
I've seen her naked a thousand times. This is different
though, and I keep my eyes averted.

The shower is hot and hard. It raises bruises on her chest.
She washes herself and crawls out onto the floor. She pulls
her nightgown on again and I help her to bed. She's too
young for this. She should be smiling and gathering
wildflowers instead of waiting for the darkness to come take
her away for good.

Living with Fear

There is a creek running through the park. There are ducks
and geese swimming against the slow current. She stands on
the bridge watching them up end themselves looking for
something to eat. She smokes and waits and waits and waits.

He comes out of the trees with his cap pulled low over his
eyes. Sunlight gives him headaches. He wears tinted glasses
and walks like a blind man, his feet feeling the ground
before putting his whole weight on it.

They kiss and turn toward the water. Their hands brush each
other, seeking familiar ground. They haven't seen each other
in months. They're awkward again and shy. They don't
know what to do with each other. It was easier talking on the
phone or writing letters.

Now that he's home, they spend hours and hours talking.
Did you kill anyone? She asks. He shrugs. He doesn't like to
think about it. *I don't know*, he says. *I just fired toward the
bullets. I did the best I could.* She leans into him and puts her
head on his shoulder. *I'm sorry,* she says.

He shakes his head. It doesn't matter. He's home now and he
has all of the time in the world. Bright lights and rumbling
sounds make him jumpy and defensive, but it'll pass. He's
convinced himself that it'll pass. He hopes she will be there
when he's less afraid, more of a man.

Fear of Open Spaces

I saw your face in a dream last night. I slept and dreamed of you. You'd grown old. Your eyes were nearly invisible in a mass of bags and wrinkles. Your hands were gnarled and weak. *Shh,* you said. *It's okay.*

Today, you come home. You come home and I wrap you in my arms and kiss your tired eyes. You go to the bedroom and unpack. You lie on the bed and rest until suppertime. I've started a roast.

I let you rest, but I find reasons to keep coming into the bedroom to look at your face, the way your hands cross on your belly. You're beautiful when you sleep, and you're home where I can watch over you. Nothing bad can happen. I'll stand guard over you.

You wake and change your clothes. You come to the kitchen, wrap your arms around me, and kiss the back of my neck. *I told you,* you say. *Nothing happened.* I shrug you off and set the potatoes on the counter. *You still should've stayed,* I say. *I didn't want you to go.*

After supper, I let you wash the dishes. I light a cigarette and pour myself a glass of wine. *You never listen to me,* I say. *I listen,* you say. *But I have to work too.* That's the whole point. Your job is more important than doing what your husband asks.

We sit together in the living room, holding hands, fighting quietly. It's impossible to throw things and yell when you're holding hands. *I wanted you to stay,* I say. *I needed you.* You frown and your hand pulls away. *I can't just not work,* you say.

But why? I ask. *I'm important too.* Now you take your hand from mine. You pull away and you take a long time to say

64

something. Anger makes you quiet. You're quiet now. *We have to eat,* you say. *You have buy clothes to wear and there's roof over our head.*

Angry now, you leave me sitting on the couch. I watch you pace. It's just a thought. It's just something I need. Can you see the difference between hypochondria and fear? I'm afraid for you all of the time. I cannot bring you home again if you die in the field. I cannot save you.

It's safe, you say. *Nothing's going to happen.* I nod and light a cigarette. *Okay,* I say. I give in, but I know what I know. Bad things happen every day. I don't know how she does it. All the people. All the cars. All the ways to die when you leave the house.

Anniversary Trip

We stop in Portland for coffee. We stop and use the bathroom and drink coffee on our way to the beach. The beach calls us with salt and sand. My lover sits at a table near the window staring at the cars in the parking lot. *I can't wait,* she says. *The gulls, the starfish, the wind.* I come back from the counter and sit with her while she sips her coffee. I go out for a cigarette.

The world is close here. The buildings rise up and scratch at the sky, hoping to uncover something. No one knows what.

Back in the car, the radio plays Cole Porter. The backseat is loaded with our gear, our tent, our clothes, a gas stove to cook eggs and fish. The mountains here are green. The day is clear and grows cooler the closer we get to the ocean.

What about sharks? My lover asks. *There are sharks in the water.*

I don't know what to say. Maybe we'll stay out of the water. Maybe we'll just stand on the tide-hardened sand and watch the surf pound the rocks waiting for us to climb them.

We can walk on the beach, collecting agates if you like, I say. *I like agates,* she says. She smiles and her teeth are white against her pale lips. She closes her eyes for a few minutes. She smiles and I wonder what she's thinking. I wonder why she's so happy now, on the way to the sea.

Weight of Sadness

Late in the morning, the bells ring from the church down the street. She stands in the street waving down cars. No one stops. No one helps her. She bleeds from a slash in her wrist, a wound open and red. Someone blows their horn at her, yells at her to get out of the street. People begin to gather and someone calls the police. The police come and they call the paramedics who take their time getting through the city. No one is dying. This is not a medical emergency.

They take her to the hospital and the doctor stitches up the cut. *Were you trying to die?* They ask. She looks at her feet, embarrassed. *It seemed like a good idea,* she says. They leave her in a room and come back with scrubs. They take her clothes and give her a nicotine patch to curb the cravings. She waits alone in a little room. Nurses come and check on her, but no one says anything. They hold onto her until a bed opens on the fifth floor.

The halls are pale and decorated with safe landscapes and abstracts. She walks to the big metal door to the psych ward. Inside, they keep the people without a reason to live. Inside, they keep the voices that make her miserable. There's nothing she can do here. She'll walk the ward and stare out the windows at the parking garage and the freeway. She'll do her best to get through this, but her sadness is heavy. Her sadness weighs on her like a blanket of water pushing her down to the floor and pinning her there.

Wednesday Night Service

We walked through the church on a Wednesday night. The
night the youth group met, but there was no one here yet.
The walls echoed with our steps. The windows hung
curtained in the dusk. Outside, summer heat made the day
heavy and wet. We turned on the air conditioning and made
out in the Sunday school. When the pastor arrived, we pulled
our shirts on and fingered our hair into place. The pastor
trusted us with a key and we took advantage of that trust.

You can't tell anyone, she says. I wouldn't dare. I wouldn't
even tell my pastor to whom I tell everything. She arranges
her face for the pastor when he comes through the big doors
facing the street. We set up the chairs in the meeting room
and listen to the air conditioner rattle out cool air.

What're you up to? The pastor asks. We shrug and look at
the floor. *Just thought we'd help set up,* I say. *Bless you,* the
pastor says, not knowing the real reason, we're here, not
knowing that we were looking for a place to explore our
bodies.

Failure to Make Rent

There's water here, water from the sky, water running through the gutters to the downspout at the corner of the building. Fear thrills through my belly. I have no secrets except that I cannot pay my rent and the landlords will go after my ex, because she signed the lease to get me in her. I call her and try to tell her, but there is only so much I can say and I can't say this.

When she comes over, she says she's taking the money from my next Disability check. She asks what happened. *Bad book keeping,* I say. *I lost track.* She shakes her head. *You have to do better than that,* she says. I huddle under my shoulders and wait for the yelling, but she doesn't yell. *I'll take care of it,* she says and I say I'm sorry. She leaves then, not interested in sorry. Now that she's gone, I think about suicide. I think of the pills I keep in my bedroom. But the shame of the act keeps me from doing anything. I cannot kill myself. I have my sons to think about. I have my mother and father. I am not alone in this world even if no one calls to talk to me. Whatever I do reaches out and changes people. Whatever I do changes the wind of existence.

Fun

I remember being young and full of fire. I was loud. People didn't figure into my world. She was older than I was. Her hair waved in the wind. She wore blue eye shadow and her lips were red as fresh blood. I met her at a dance and we spoke for a while, but then she left and I never learned her name. Later, days later, she was on the street smoking a cigarette. I went to her and asked if she would give me her name, something to remember her by. She laughed and said people called her Mike. I didn't know what was so funny, except her name, but I let it go. Mike gave me her phone number and that night I called her, asked if she would like to go a movie, somewhere dark and quiet.

We went to the movie and sat in the darkness, close to each other. She smelled of myrrh and smoke. Halfway through the film, her hand reached out for mine. We sat there like that for over an hour. When the lights came up, she smiled and led me into the night. We talked of everything. I told her that I'd never been in love. Her face went still. *This isn't love,* she said. *This is just fun.*

Party

It begins without her. The music blares out the windows into the wet night air. The walls dance. The light plays on the muddy grass. When she arrives, the party is well under way. She wears a blue dress like wearing the summer sky. Her hair is braided and falls down along her spine. She lights a cigarette and enters the crowd. No one knows her. She has only one friend and her friend has already left with a woman she'd met.

The food in the corner is rich and savory. She eats and watches the dancers on the floor. She drinks beer until she is comfortable talking with strangers. The night is heavy with smoke and shadows. Paper arches decorate the walls. She dances with a man named Elias. Elias tries to get her into a corner where he can kiss her neck, where she can't back away.

She leaves after an hour. She has nothing in common with these people. The music is too loud, the men too made up for her comfort. She goes home, washes away the smell of cigarette smoke, and fried meat. She lies in bed wondering why she can't seem to enjoy herself when there are people around.

Things a Son Can't Ask

I imagine her combing her hair. I imagine her sitting on the
edge of her bed, running a brush through it. My father
always loved her hair. He would smell it when he came into
the room. He would stroke it when they sat together on the
couch. She would comb it and he would lie in bed watching
her. She would braid it before coming to bed, to keep it out
of her face. He'd kiss her neck then and she would hum.
They would make love, the floor creaking with each thrust. I
would hide my head in my pillows, my room next to theirs.
In the morning, I'd stare at them and wonder how they could
seem so normal after a night of sex. I would stare at their
faces and they'd smile, but they kept their secrets and this
isn't something a son asks about.

Heaviness

Last night, in the moonlight, she lit a cigarette and offered it to me. We sat in the park watching the stars burn blue and white. We watched the moon through the branches. The day's heat had softened to a gentle evening. In the morning, the grass would wake wet with dew. We smoked and held each other and after an hour, we went home. We made pastrami sandwiches on rye bread and sat at the table, listening to the walls around us settle into the foundation. *Is this what you thought it would be?* She asked. I shake my head. *Nothing's what it seems.*

When we went to bed, we made love. We flowed into each other, our sweat mingling. When we finished she rolled away from me and closed her eyes. I curled around her back and held her until she slept. After she slept I rose, dressed, and wandered out to the living room, to the balcony and I watched the night grow old.

I wrote in my journal. *I cannot sleep,* I wrote. *Anne is peaceful and I am restless. The night is heavy and I cannot move.*

Her Father's Funeral

The rain knocks the petals to the ground and kicks them around the parking lot. Wind makes tiny pink tornadoes. She wears a black dress on her way to her father's funeral. The day is perfect for a funeral, gray and miserable.

At the church, she kneels and says the rosary. She prays for his soul. The priest says Mass and people stare down at her father's dead face before they go to the cemetery for the burial.

There are chairs set up next to the grave. An awning keeps the rain off, but the wind cuts right through the crowd. After the final prayers, everyone gathers at her mother's house with food and conversation. *He was a good man,* someone says. She shakes her head. These people did not know her father. They did not know his secrets. They did not know that he would hold her in his lap and grind himself against her crotch. They did not know about the night he came to her room and fell asleep on top of her.

It's over now. He's dead and people think he was a good man. She wants to scream out the secrets, but she keeps them instead. They are her secrets now. Only hers. He's dead now and she must keep the face of propriety.

Final Meal

What'll you do without me? She asks. We sit together in the restaurant eating soup from ceramic cups. *I don't know,* I say. *I'll figure something out.* Her eyebrows raise and she frowns. *Am I that toxic?* She asks. I shake my head. I put down the spoon and lean in close. *I don't trust you,* I say. *I love you, but I don't trust you.* She cries when I say it. *I'll do better,* she says. *You can't just leave.* I go back to my soup and watch her dab at her eyes with the napkin. *I can't,* I say. *I'm tired.*

She looks sad here, at our last meal together. I want to make her smile again, but I can't. I'm leaving and there is no reason to smile. I'll miss her. I'll mourn her, but I won't come back. It's over now. I'll fall in love with someone else, but it'll take time. I don't fall that easily.

I have to go, she says. *I can't do this.* She sets her spoon down and rises. *I'm sorry,* she says. *If that means anything.* She's always sorry, but now it's not enough.

When she's gone, I sit alone in the restaurant, waiting for her to come back. I want to change my mind, but she's gone and there's nothing here to save my marriage. There's nothing here to look forward to. I'll be fine without her, but right now, it tears at me, a dog breaking through the grass after a rabbit, tearing it apart with fangs, jaws, and claws.

The Hooker and Her Son

She works the street corner where the cops come looking for hookers. She fucks in cars in alleyways and parks. She works the street all night, spending her day with her son who goes to school in the fall. She's not slept more than an hour or two at a time for months. Her ex calls and gives her grief over visitations. He wants more time with his son. She makes him promise to keep his drugs away. He must, *must*, be sober the entire time. He promises and she takes his word for it. She lets him take the boy, who looks forward to seeing his father.

She sleeps all day and works all night. She is wet and cold, only warm when in strangers' cars. A cop stops her on the street. *What're you doing?* The cop asks. *Nothing,* she says. *Do nothing at home.*

She walks away, but comes back after the cop has gone on his patrol. She works until the traffic peters out and there are no more men. She goes home and sleeps and late in the day, she picks her son up. He takes a cigarette out of her pack and lights it. *What're you doing?* She asks. *You and Daddy do it,* he says. *Put it out,* she says. Her son tosses the butt out the window and she worries about him. Smoking is the smallest thing. What'll happen if he sees more?

Every Night

These walls keep the rain out. When the clouds break,
sunshine pours through the windows warming the benches
set into the walls. She comes and talks to me in the Common
Room. We talk of rape. She tells me about the man who
drugged her and raped her in a bathroom stall. She tells me
of coming to, finding herself surrounded by men staring
down at her naked body. Someone called the cops and the
cops took her to the emergency room. They did a rape kit,
gathering the particular evidence. *I cried and cried and
cried,* she says.

When she found out she was pregnant, she cried some more.
She didn't know what to do. She didn't want this baby. She
made an appointment and the baby went away. She spent
hours every day in the shower. She startled at noises and
cried herself to sleep at night. That's why she's here. She
cried herself to sleep every night.

Storm

Hail beats the muddy earth. Wind pushes it sideways into the trees, tearing the leaves just open there. Samantha holds her umbrella up and huddles in a corner waiting for it to pass. This is just a little storm, a reminder of what could be.

Samantha walks out of the corner when the hail peters out ten minutes later. Hail never lasts long here. Cars are dinged and scratched. Samantha runs her hand over one ruined surface after another. She says a little prayer and moves on.

The window in her kitchen is broken when she gets home. Nothing is missing or moved. No one had gotten in. It was the hail and the wind. She calls her landlord and tells her about the window. *I'll be out tomorrow,* she says. In the meantime, Samantha hangs a sheet over it.

Rapist

Late last night, I did her laundry while she slept. I folded shirts blue as a choked man and jeans worn through at the cuffs. She wears her jeans long and the cuffs always wear through. I put clothes quietly into drawers and stood at the foot of the bed watching her sleep.

She wakes and startles. Her eyes get big for a second and she scrambles away from me. *I thought you were a rapist,* she says. I shrug. *I could be,* I say. She shakes her head. *You could never be a rapist,* she says. *You don't want that kind of power.*

I go out to the couch and lie down. I lie down and close my eyes. I don't want that kind of power. I don't want to hurt anyone. I want to sleep. I want to close my eyes and float away, but I can't. My mind spins a thousand webs of thought. My mind clatters like bones in a cup, waiting to tell the future.

Cruel Words

She says things she doesn't mean. The words just come and they fall from her mouth before she can bite down on them with her teeth. She doesn't mean to hurt anyone, but she does and now people avoid her.

Sitting alone in the arbor, on a wrought iron bench, she smokes a cigarette and waits for a stranger to come sit with her. Hours pass and no one comes. The sun is going down and she has no one to talk to. She walks home in the dark. She eats a bowl of soup and gets ready for bed.

It's too early for bed. The stars are young in the night. She goes to bed and thinks about all of the people that she's hurt with her words. She doesn't know how to heal the wounds she's opened. If she could say she's sorry, she would, but no one is listening, no one cares.

Her son calls. *Are you angry?* He asks. She shakes her head, forgetting that he cannot see her. *Mom?* He asks. *I'm fine,* she says. *Just lonely.* Her son breathes into the receiver. *I'll be home soon,* he says. *You can tell me all about it.*

Verdict

Warm milk pours from the ruptured jug. She stands in the kitchen crying. The sunlight pours through the window and she doesn't know what to do. *What's next?* She asks. I stand across the room watching her. *I don't know*, I say.

She mops the mess up with a dishtowel and flings it into the sink. Her hands are gnarled and bent. She's too young for this kind of pain. It wracks through the muscles in her forearms. She takes Percocet for it and sleeps away the morning.

Rachel, I call. *Rachel, wake up.*

Her dreams wash away and she opens one eye. She frowns and pulls the comforter up over her mouth. *Don't look at me,* she says.

The doctor called, I say. *She wants to see you.*

We drive to the office through town. We wait for the doctor and read *The New Yorker* in the waiting room. They call us back.

The cancer has spread, the doctor says. *It's gone to your brain.*

How much time? Rachel asks.

I hate to put limits, the doctor says. *You should make the best of what you have.*

We walk into the sunshine. Rachel looks around the world, the trees with their fresh green leaves, the crows calling from the sky.

I hope rains on the day I die, she says. *No one should go out when it's this beautiful.*

Waiting for Consummation

The river runs cold and hard here. We wade up to our knees feeling the water pull at us like a child seeking attention for a trick she's about to perform perfectly for the first time. We stand barefoot in the gravel, the salmon swimming past us on their way to the perfect breeding shallows far up stream. An eagle waits in a snag not far away waiting for a chance at one, but she and I command this portion of the river and the salmon get a free pass.

Do you believe in heaven? She asks. I close my eyes and think about my answer. *In a way,* I say. *I believe there is more to the universe than science. I believe in magic.* She nods and lights a cigarette. She blows smoke into the foggy mountains air. *I believe in the never-ending soul,* she says. *I believe in an ultimate reward.* That's why she has her own tent and will not sleep with me. She has morals. They stand in the way of taking the next step.

At dinner, she prays, quietly, without me. I watch without partaking. We eat fish, mushrooms, and leeks fried in a cast iron skillet with butter. She sits close to the fire, her face red and black in the night. *Can this be heaven?* I ask. She stops and stares at me. *Don't make fun,* she says. *I'm not,* I say. *I'm just curious.*

We kill the fire and hurry to our tents. I lie in my sleeping bag, thinking this would be nicer if we could make love like the adults we are.

I'm half-asleep when the tent flap opens. *Nothing's going to happen,* she says. *I'm just cold.* We curl around each other and one hand brushes a breast. Maybe tomorrow she'll show me the whole thing. Maybe tomorrow, we'll consummate the relationship.

Sincerity

This one is my daughter, she says and points to a photo on the wall. *This one is my father with his father*, she says. *I loved my grandfather.*

This is the first time I've been to her place. I walk along the walls looking the photos, the paintings, the drawings hung there. She walks with me, telling me the stories behind the images.

We stop in the bedroom. *This is my bed*, she says and then she stops talking. We stand at the foot of the bed, staring at each other. She has something to say, but the words just aren't there.

Slowly, we get naked. We make love full of kisses. Her nails leave tracks in my shoulders. She bites my neck. She moans and bucks. When we're done, she smiles. *Thanks*, she says.

She's always so sincere.

Voices

Her flesh is silver in the sunlight. She dances naked in the
street until the police come and wrap her in a blanket, and
cuff her wrists behind her back. They say she doesn't have a
grip on reality, but maybe she does. Maybe she knows
something we don't. Maybe the voices tell her things we can
never hear.

In the hospital, they dress her in scrubs and leave her in a
little white room in the back of the emergency department.
The nurse brings her a warm blanket. She paces the room
and talks to the walls. The doctors ask her questions, but she
can only answer some of them.

Come morning, they take her upstairs and feed her pills.
They feed her pills and the pills kill the voices. The voices
die and she's alone now. For days, there is silence. When
they let her go, she can't live with the quiet. She's gotten
used to the noise. She sits on the edge of the freeway with
the traffic's white noise washing over her. She has nowhere
to go and no one to tell her the secrets of the world.

She Dies in Clarity

On the outskirts, Amanda stands in the mud, watching the heron hunting for frogs and fish. She lights a cigarette. She waits for her lover to come get her. She can't remember the way home. She tends to forget her way in this new town, this new house.

Amanda comes home and sits in the dark while her lover goes back to work. Fifty years he's taken care of her. Fifty years they've loved one another. Now her memory is slipping away, water through sand. Right now, she knows something is wrong, but she cannot name it. She knows she'll die surrounded by strangers. She'll die alone in a bed with white sheets and beige blankets. First, she'll lose everyone she loves. First, she'll lose herself.

Amanda kills herself when her mind clears. She swallows the pills and lies in bed waiting, waiting for the darkness to fold over her. She pukes in her sleep. Her lover finds her and calls for help, but there is no help. Amanda is dead. For a moment there, she saw the future.

The Reliable Stranger

I'll love you forever, she says. *If you buy me a beer.* Drunk
already, she begged drinks from every man in the bar. It
worked too. Men bought her drinks and she sat with them
with her arm around their shoulders, flirting and whispering
in their ears. One man she takes out to the parking lot and
comes back twenty bucks richer.

She sits at my table and puts her head in her arms, her eyes
closes, swaying in her seat. Time for her to go home. *Where
do you live?* I ask. She moans something. I don't know what.
Where?

I don't know.

I live two blocks away and I decide to take her there. I help
her up and we walk out into the rain. We stop on the corner
for her to puke in the holly bushes there. Once home, I lay
her on the couch and take her shoes off. *I need a shower,* she
says. It's a bad idea, but she insists, so I take her to the
bathroom and she strips out of her clothes. I turn on the
water, lukewarm, hoping to sober her up a bit. She gets in
and I go out to the living room.

I wait and wait and nothing happens. The shower's white
noise carries all the way through the walls to me. I let
twenty, thirty minutes pass before checking on her. I hadn't
heard her fall, but anything was possible.

She's passed out in the tub. I turn the water off, lift her wet
body out of the tub, and drag her to the couch. I lay her on
her belly and throw a blanket over her. I get her clothes and
put them on the floor next to the couch. I go to bed.

In the morning, I wake before she does. I wake, she sleeps,
and I make coffee and eggs with potatoes and toast with real

butter. *Where are my clothes?* She calls. *On the floor,* I say. *Don't look.*

I stay in the kitchen and she finally joins me. *What's your name?* She asks. *Larry,* I say. *Did we fuck, Larry?* I shake my head. *No.* She looks me up and down. *I was naked.* I shrug. *You took a shower and passed out.*

We eat at the table and she lights a cigarette. *Where are we?* She asks. *My apartment. Do you know where you live?* She frowns. *B Street,* she says. *You sure we didn't fuck?* I nod. *I have to go,* she says and gets her shoes.

She's gone now. I fold the blanket and light a cigarette. Maybe we should've fucked. Maybe I should've been something other than the reliable stranger, the gentleman to those in need.

Forever and Ever

All winter you kept me warm. All night you held me and in the morning, we made love. We showered together and shared breakfast at the kitchen table. We walked into the day and watched the birds and squirrels in the trees. We smoked cigarettes and held onto each other, pooling our body heat. We walked and walked and walked. Flowers began to unfurl, the petals the only color in a sepia world. I picked a crocus from the edge of the sidewalk and slid it behind your ear. You smiled at me. *Forever and ever,* I said. You touched my face. *Forever and ever.*

Cruelty

The words come without warning or thought. The look on
your face when I say them is heartbreaking. I didn't mean to
hurt your feelings, but I was angry. I say things when I'm
angry and they always come back to me, harsh and bitter.
Later I'll feel bad, right now I just want you to leave me be.

It was all about money. You didn't want me using the credit
card for cigarettes and beer. *It's for emergencies,* you said.
But I paid the bills. I figured I could use it for what I wanted.
You didn't yell or cuss. You just asked me to leave the card
home when I went to the store.

I knew it wasn't right, but I had no cash and I couldn't go
without my addictions. When you asked me to lay off the
card, I said the first thing that came to mind.

You're not fat and I'm not cruel. Then if you weren't fat, the
words wouldn't have hurt so much and if I weren't cruel,
they wouldn't have come at all.

Virgin

She is perfect. I think of her all day. At night, she comes to the apartment and we drink bourbon from short glasses and smoke cigarettes on the patio. I wait for her to touch me, but we haven't gotten there yet. She only stays a few hours before walking away into the darkness.

There is room for her in my bed, but she's never used it. I have yet to see her naked. I have yet to do more than place a hand on her waist while we kiss. She's shy about sex and I can wait. *When you're ready,* I say. She smiles. *You're a good man,* she says. I don't know about that.

At dinner, she says she's ready. She will not look at me, but she says she'll stay the night. The thought of it thrills me. I've wanted her for so long. I've waited for this for weeks. She drinks her bourbon and gets another. She lights a cigarette and stands on the patio, a shadow under the stars.

I take it slow. I pet and stroke. I kiss her neck, her breasts, and her thighs. I ease myself into her and she moans a little moan. There is blood, but only a little. I move with caution and she arcs her back. Afterwards, she smiles at me. *That was nice,* she says. Nice? It was best I'd ever had.

Done

Dust and pollen float through the summer air in thick banks shifting in the wind like a curtain. I look for Lily in the bars along Main Street. I look for her in the parks. I walk through town stopping in her favorite places, but she is not there.

Last night we fought and she stormed out of the house. I went to bed and slept, but she never came home. Now I'm worried. She's never been gone this long. She needs to come home. I need her to be safe. I look for her, but she can't be found.

Her phone goes to voicemail and I leave message after message. I go home, hoping she's there waiting for me. She's not though. She's nowhere to be found. The police won't look for her until she's been gone a whole day. I sit in the living room, smoking, and making up vicious scenarios. I see Lily's body in the wetlands at the edge of town. I see her dumped in the street, bloody and hurt. I don't know what's going on. I miss her already.

She comes home in the afternoon. Her clothes are wrinkled and she smells of beer and cigarettes, a man's cologne. *Where have you been?* I ask. She stares at me and shrugs. *Out,* she says. *I went to the bar,* she says. *I met someone who loves me.* I don't know what that means and Lily will say no more. She showers and changes her clothes. She leaves again. A man waits in a car for her and they drive away. What do I do now? Is it over between us, or is this just a test? I wait the whole night through and decide that this is it. I won't play this game. I pack some clothes and move into a motel. I leave Lily a note. *If you want to talk, call me. Otherwise I'm done.*

She Leaves without Me

I wake before her and watch her sleep. I watch the curve of
her breast rising into her arm, the long run of one thigh. I
watch the angle of her jaw. Taking her nipple into my
mouth, I listen to her moan, wondering what she's dreaming
of now.

She rolls away from me and I put one hand on her hip,
cuddling close to her back. For an hour, I drift in and out of
sleep like that. Then the alarm cries and she rises into the
gray morning light. I watch her walk to the bathroom and
listen to the shower sing. I get up and make coffee, waiting
for her to come to me.

She sits in the kitchen and eats toast. Her teeth are perfect.
Her hands are sure and quick. *I'll miss you,* I say. *It's only
eight hours,* she says and gets up, ready to go. She kisses me
and I walk her to the car. She drives away and I worry I'll
never see her again. I could call, but I don't want to be
clingy.

Back inside, I clean the dishes and wipe away the crescent
print of her lipstick from the coffee cup.

Looking for my Lover Who Left Last Night

Night comes and the lights on the street glow ivory. I stand
in the rain looking through windows, looking for my girl.
She left me last night. She packed her things and walked out,
going somewhere. I didn't want to follow her then, but I do
now. I want to follow her, touch her hand, and tell her I'm
sorry for being such an ass. I ignored her when she was with
me because I thought she'd always be with me. I never
thought she'd leave. Last night, she said she found someone
who doesn't ignore her. It's hard to imagine her with
someone else. I want to bring her back to the apartment. I'll
cook dinner and apologize. I'll be more attentive.

She's gone though. I don't know where she went. I walk the
streets and look through the windows for her red hair. I look
for her narrow jaw, the slope of her neck. She's nowhere.
She's everywhere. I imagine I see her in every window, but
then I look again and she's not there.

Come midnight, the lights go off in the houses. The people
there pull their curtains closed. I go home and lie alone in
my bed, but I cannot sleep. Where is she? I worry about her.
I love her now that she's gone. This is how it works. Lovers
split after years and one pines over the loss while the other
lives a new life.

The Girl in the Store

I stare at her in the store, hoping for a chance to have a few words. She stops at the onions in the produce section and picks out a few Walla Walla Sweets. She walks to the butcher's counter. I follow her without following her. I want to ask her name, but I don't know how to approach her without looking like a stalker. She lifts a roast out of the display and goes to the checkout counter. I watch her pay and walk out of the store. I hurry to the parking lot, but she's gone now, dissipated in the summer breeze. I wonder if I'll see her again. I wonder if she'll smile at me when I run my cart into hers just to break the ice.

The Question You Should Never Ask

They looked at each other's faces. A candle burned between them. They sat quietly talking about love. No one bothered them, but the waiter who brought more wine. *Do you love me?* Kelly asked. Lorn saw her eyes. He saw the way her hands folded around the stem of her wine glass. He wanted a cigarette, but this was a non-smoking restaurant. *I'm getting there,* he said. Tears welled up in Kelly's eyes. She loved Lorn, but he was slow coming to the point. What was she supposed to do now? How could she go on loving him if he wasn't with her yet?

After supper, they walked to the car and rode home silently. Kelly wanted to say something, but she didn't know what. She wanted to make Lorn love her, but she didn't know how. Love comes on its own time.

Home now, Kelly goes straight to bed and Lorn sits in his chair writing in his journal.

I think I hurt Kelly tonight, he wrote. *I don't know how to love such a beautiful woman.*

Gardening on Sunday

Jennifer kneels in the garden amongst the irises pulling
weeds and spreading slug bait. She smokes a cigarette with
squinted eyes. Her husband stands barefoot in the loose soil
and lifts the bucket full of weeds, carrying it to the garbage
near the garage. They do this every Sunday. They work side
by side, not talking, just tending to the yard and garden.
Later, he puts his shoes on and mows the lawn. At the end of
the day, they sit together on the couch, holding hands,
exhausted from so much sunlight, from the manual labor.
They'll shower together and watch television until midnight
when they go to bed and dream of ants and the rose bush's
ragged leaves.

Children

Looking down from her balcony, Renee learns about her neighbor's pregnancy. The neighbor was on the phone with her mother and Renee was out smoking a cigarette, not meaning to eavesdrop, but hearing every word. Still she stood there long after her cigarette burned out and listened, remembering her own pregnancy, remembering the early years of bringing up a baby. Her kids are grown now, married, making their own families. She gets her phone and calls her son. It goes to voicemail, but even that sliver of his voice is comforting. She calls again just to hear it. *It's Mom,* she says. *Call me.* She closes the phone and stares out at the houses on the street wondering at the children playing the yards. Do their mothers love them the way she loves her kids? Are they safe? Renee weeps a little at the thought of tragedy. It waits in the street, ready to take a child's life if no one is watching. So Renee watches. She stands on her balcony overseeing the kids in the neighborhood. She doesn't know their names, but she watches over them all the same. Children are sacred. They make the walls of loneliness bearable.

Night Routine

Killing time slowly. Waiting for the sun to go down before
getting into bed and nodding through the night. She makes
supper and hums in the kitchen. Her lover comes and kisses
the rim of her ear. They stand like that, his arms around her
waist for a long moment before the water boils, ready for the
rice she's making.

He calls her name when the water stops boiling. She comes
to the table wet from steam rising from the stove. He takes
her breasts in his hands, kneading each one with his thin, dry
fingers. She holds him close, making a promise with her
body, until he rolls away and goes out for a cigarette.

In the middle of the night, she wakes from a nightmare and
lies in the dark listening to the wind in the screens, her
lover's heavy breath. She goes into the kitchen for a cigarette
and a glass of water. The nightmare fades and she's back in
bed again, waiting for morning, hoping for sleep.

Fear

I want to touch her body with my tongue. I want to wrap up in my arms and hold her until she stops trembling. I want to kiss her shoulder blades. Her fingertips touch my face like the kiss of snow. Her eyes water when she talks of her father's death. Her children will never know what it's like to sit on his lap and listen to him tell stories of growing up in the woods.

She never stays the night. She leaves in the hours before dawn and drives home to her children and sends them to their day before going to bed again and resting through the sunlit hours. *We could get married,* I say. She shakes her head. *Never again,* she says. *Never again.*

I want to hold her in the morning after her children have left for the day. I want lie down with her and guard her sleep. I want to be in love, but love has nothing to do with it. *I'm scared,* she says. I stroke her hair and tell her it's okay. I'm scared too.

Casual Sex

There are secrets in the hours after midnight. Traffic on the street is a bass roar. I bring Trish home one night after drinking. She stumbles through the room looking for the secrets I keep. We drink again, bourbon and water. We pour ourselves out and share the air when we kiss. The anticipation of sex is thrilling.

Her breasts brush my arm and she looks me in the eye. Her lips part and our tongues scrape on teeth. Naked and cold, we make love until the blankets are heavy and warm on our bare hips. She doesn't stay the night. She dresses and walks out to the door. I wrap myself in a robe and lock it behind her. Back in bed, I revel in the smell of her. I lie there and wish she'd slept over, but she never stays the night. *I'm not looking for love*, she said when I asked her about it. I shouldn't have brought her home. I want more than casual sex, but a few hours of warmth is better than a night spent completely alone.

This is How it Works

This street is perfect. Houses rise up from green lawns and the sidewalks are unbroken. Ed and I walk hip-to-hip, arms wrapped tight around our waists, holding on as if the wind would lift us up and carry us out to sea.

We sit in the park and watch the children play. Crows call back and forth, collecting shiny trash to line their nests. I light a cigarette and share it with Ed. Her lips fold around the filter, light as wings. Her hands are warm and dry. Her shoulders strong and wide. I love her shoulders, the junction of neck and back. I kiss her there and she leans into me as if I were a wall holding her up forever.

Later, I'll go to work. I'll think of her all night and stumble from task to task. In the morning, I'll slip into bed with her while she sleeps, careful not to shake her out of her dreams. She'll roll over then, presenting her back. I'll curl around it and drift away.

This is how it works. This is what means to be in love, the constant pressure of skin on skin. The inability to think of anything other than the woman waiting for you at home.

This Is What It's About

Irene brings a bottle of wine and lilies for the table. She kisses me and puts on some music, something light and lovely. She pulls me to the middle of the floor and we dance. I'm awkward and shy. The windows are all open and the curtains pulled back. Anyone can see me if they bothered to look, but Irene doesn't care. She wants to dance so we dance.

When she gets tired, she sits on the couch and closes her eyes. Shadows are forming around her mouth, under her chin. She lights a cigarette and drinks wine. I sit with her and rest my head on her shoulder.

Night comes late and we eat in the kitchen. We eat in the kitchen and talk about the weekend. Maybe we'll go to the lake and swim in the green water, floating for a while before sinking into the deep with the bass and trout. Maybe we'll walk from gallery to gallery, looking at paintings and vases, nude sculptures and glassware. I don't know what we'll do, but I know I'll wake late in the morning and wait for her to rise from her dreams so I can offer her coffee and eggs. This is what it's about, wine and music, sex and eggs.

Living Alone

For a while, she lived alone. The whispering house was her only companion. She didn't know what to say to the walls, so she just listened, trying to figure out the words. Before he left, he told her he was in love with someone else. She cried all night. He slept on the couch. She couldn't do anything, so she helped him pack, and watched him drive away on the wet street.

She got a smaller place and settled into a routine of work and sleep. She stopped eating and whittled herself down to a bone. At night, she drank wine, smoked cigarettes, and thought about her loneliness. Meeting someone was impossible. She didn't know what to say or do. She didn't know how to flirt. She wanted love, but didn't know how to find it.

On the weekend, she cleaned her apartment. She met the man in the laundry room. He lived across the way. They talked of things. They reveled in each other's company. When it was time to go, the shook hands and she wishes she had more time to give him. She wished she had something to lure him home. But the day was over and she went home to her empty place.

They first dated a month later. They had dinner with a bottle of wine and they came home to her place and drank another before making love. She wasn't normally this fast, but she wanted someone to touch her. She wanted someone to admire her body. It didn't matter that she didn't know him well enough to have sex with him.

When he slept, she slipped out to the balcony and smoked. She stood in the wind and watched the stars and moon spinning through the night. She didn't know how to say she loved him. It was too soon. The words might scare him off.

She wanted him to stay forever. She wanted whatever he had to offer. If he left now, she might never get back on her feet.

Death Ruined Everything

A light cuts through the fog and darkness, but the rain makes it hazy, indistinct. Irene smokes a cigarette. She sits on her patio and watches the night. Her children are sleeping and she thinks about slipping down to the store for a bottle of wine. She has not met a man she could love since her husband died. The men in her life are brittle and touchy. She wants a strong man. She wants a man who will hold her after sex and whisper away the sadness filling her life.

She checks on the children and undresses in her bedroom. Her children are getting older. Soon they'll leave and she'll have the apartment to herself. Loneliness scares her. What will she do when they're gone? Will she disappear all together? Will she fade away?

In the morning, she makes waffles and bacon and sits at the table with her kids. They eat silently. No one has words this early. After breakfast, they wander down to the bus stop and wait for their day to begin. She sits in the kitchen, the dishes around her. She cleans and thinks of all the years she could've had, but death ruined everything.

Split Between Love and Obligation

Consider falling in love, the fall of heat in the summer. She makes do with who she has now, but she has taken a lover too. Her husband is not a bad man. He just doesn't have anything to say to her anymore. Her lover makes her smile. They walk long walks. They make love in his bed and talk about going someplace with a bridge so they can stare into the broken water watching the light reflect. Her husband has moved to the couch. They don't even pretend to be married. Divorce is expensive though. In a couple of years, they'll end what they started, but right now, there is nothing they can do.

Move in with me, her lover says. She shakes her head. There are the children to consider. Moving would throw them into a fit. She can't afford a place of her own now. She has debt to consider. Still, she sleeps in her lover's bed most nights. Her husband is considerate enough never to ask where she's been. Mornings, she goes home, makes breakfast for her kids, and sends them off to school. She plays the piano in the living room while her husband works.

After dinner, she goes to her lover and leaves her husband to put the kids to bed. She sits in her lover's living room and makes coffee in his kitchen. They talk of the future. They talk of their life. *I love you,* her lover says. She puts a finger against his lips. *Don't say that,* she says. *Not yet.* She's not ready for love. She's not ready to give her life away again. Not yet. Not right now.

Their First Date

Steam rose from the asphalt in wispy tendrils like hair
twisting, joining the fog trapped between the houses on the
street. Rain was a simple mist folding and unfolding like a
curtain in an open window. Iris and Ben came home, hip to
hip, from dinner and a bottle of wine. They laughed, sang,
and stumbled on the broken sidewalk. They opened another
bottle and drank the dark wine, sitting in the kitchen talking
of love. They kissed and their hands played over their
bodies. Making love on the couch was awkward and
dangerous. Afterwards they lay belly to back, moist of sweat
and sex. Midnight came and Iris rose in a rush, gathering her
clothes and heading to the bathroom. Ben watched her go.
You could stay, he said, but Iris shook her head. *The
babysitter is expecting me,* she said.

She left then, the door unlocked, the windows looking down
on the empty room. Ben lit a cigarette and wrapped himself
in a robe. He went outside and stood in the grass, wondering
if this was it, if she'd ever come back.

Inevitable

Coming home from the marriage counselor, you say you've lost all faith in me, your husband, and the man you promised to love. I don't know what to say so I drive silently along streets filled with traffic. I watch the cars around me, defensive, depressed.

You pack your things and move into a motel. I cannot sleep without you. I never wanted it to end this way, but you've made up your mind. You're leaving. You're dropping out of my life. *What can I do to change your mind?* I ask. You shrug. I hate it when you shrug like that.

In the middle of the night, I go out for a cigarette and watch the sky cloud over, burying the stars. I listen to the house creaking, the walls settling into the mud around the foundation. This place is too big for me. I need something smaller, someplace that doesn't remind me of you.

I'm here now, alone. Tomorrow we'll go to the lawyers. Tomorrow we'll split our lives and go wherever we need to go. I pack my things in the car, drive out to the edge of town, and burn my clothes. I burn the pictures of us. I burn the music we shared all through the years. An offering to god. I surrender to the inevitable.

A New Lover

Forgive me, but I've forgotten your face. You look familiar
but I can't place you. Would you like a drink while we catch
up? I'll sit with you for hours if you like and tell my story
until it stops making sense.

Yesterday, geese stood in the park near the creek and I
watched them for an hour before walking home and making
a sandwich. Do you like geese? Do you like walking? This is
what I do. This is how thing happen.

You can come to my apartment if you want. We'll kiss and
make love until the sun pinks the sky. Am I too forward? I
thought was what you wanted. I thought you were looking
for a lover. I know I was.

Dinner and Breakfast

The traffic is slow and loud. The gutters are full of water and leaves. I stand on my balcony and wait for her to come to me. She is a busy woman, but at the end of the day, she always comes to me. She sits in the kitchen and smokes cigarettes while I cook. She adds salt to the soup when I'm not looking. The clatter of her bones is the loudest noise I've ever heard. I wonder if she lives with pain. She doesn't say anything, but the look on her face is unbearable. I don't know how she lives like this.

She eats little bites. She is careful with her spoon and fork. Her teeth are white against her red lips. I want to kiss her, but she is so far away. Tonight, we'll make love on the couch. Anything to change the perspective.

Night comes and the wind rattles the screens. Rain beats a rhythm on the roof and I lie in bed listening to her breathe, listening to the world going on without us. In the morning, we'll drink coffee and eat eggs. *I have to go*, she'll say and I'll watch her rush out as if the tide was turning and she needs to catch a boat.

Breaking Up

She stands under the tree and smokes a cigarette. She drinks bourbon from a flask. The sun is a hazy wheel. She presses her bare toes into the grass. I walk through the park looking for her. We've made love by the creek running through it. We've sat naked in the moonlight, our skin pale and warm. She hides from me now. She has nothing to say. I miss her, but she says she's done with me. She says she needs a life. I don't know what that means.

Tomorrow she'll move her things out of the apartment. She'll leave me there alone and stunned. The empty rooms will remember her name. The bathroom will remember her scent. I'll walk along the walls, my hands empty, my mind circling.

When I find her again, I smile and she asks how I'm doing. I shrug. She doesn't touch me. She moves away. She stands under the tree with her cigarette and stares out at the grass as if she's already gone.

He Drinks Too Much

Sitting in the bar, the dim light, the neon signs, he listens the
country music from the jukebox, plugging quarters in it all
night. The sound keeps him from losing his mind. His ex
could walk in any moment and he'd turn away from her,
hoping she'd ignore him. It's a bitter fight, breaking up.
They were together all of his adult life. He doesn't know
how to meet women. He doesn't know how to fall in love.
So he drinks his bourbon and smokes his cigarettes,
wrinkling his nose at the smell of the grill across the room.

When the bar closes, he stumbles into the night and walks
home, dragging his feet. He fumbles with the locked door.
Inside, he is a little bit ashamed of himself. Old food
containers lie piled on the floor next to his chair. Beer bottles
gather like a tribe of glass columns in the kitchen. He
undresses and stands in the shower. The hot water sends
steam to the ceiling. Mold grows there, staining the white
walls.

In his bed, he drags one hand on the floor. He shivers in the
winter air, his breath a wisp of vapor. He closes his eyes and
hopes that he doesn't dream tonight. He always dreams of
his ex. He dreams of the good years and the bad. He just
wants to forget. When sleep comes, it comes fast and hard.
He falls away from himself, a stone dropped in water.

Comfort

You walk home to me and I wait for the hours to pass. You
bring sunlight. You wait for a while before the sun gives up
the sky. I stand on the balcony smoking a cigarette watching
for your face on the street. Your feet grow heavy and you
shuffle through the leaves falling in the breeze smelling of
dust and stone. You come through the door and I am ready
for you. I kiss your lips and make a bourbon for you.

Come suppertime, you tell me about your day, the way the
hours seemed to weigh on you the longer you worked, the
secrets you have to keep, the office politics you need to play.
After we eat, you go out to the balcony for a cigarette. I
wash the dishes and join you there, holding your hand,
offering whatever comfort I can offer. The sun falls from the
sky and we lie on the couch for a while. We make love in the
living room, leaving our clothes scattered about the floor.
When it's over you cry a little. I don't know where your
tears come from, but I hold you and we settle down to sleep.
Come midnight we stumble to the bed and lie there curled
around each other knowing that morning will come pull us
apart.

Silence

She comes home at the end of the day and sits in the kitchen
with her apron tied around her waist. I kiss her when I see
her and her eyes light up for a second before dulling again in
exhaustion. She sits and waits for the rice to finish cooking
on the stove, a bourbon in the glass on the table and a
paperback romance in her hands. I sit in the living room
writing poems and waiting for supper. We have been
together so long that the silence is comfortable with us. We
do not talk about the day. We only say what needs to be said
and nothing else. When we eat, we eat slowly and the quiet
night comes down and wraps us in shadow. After supper, we
go to the bedroom and undress, our bodies no longer secret,
comfortable in our nudity. We shower and lie in bed with the
lamp on for an hour before slipping down onto the mattress
and closing our eyes. In the morning, she'll rise before me
and leave without saying anything. I'll wake late and dress
alone. I'll go to the living room and write all the words I've
been saving for her but don't know how to say.

Save it for Morning

In the middle of the night when the rains had stopped and the clouds broke enough for a few stars to burn down on us with white light, we sat in a parked car outside my apartment. You didn't want to come up because it meant we would make love and we'd only known each other a few days. This was our first date and we spent the time spilling words over each other, leaking little bits of history without getting too personal. I wanted to know your body, but I was shy and didn't know how to say it. We sat and kissed, your hand found the center of my chest, and I could feel my heart beating against your palm. My legs and back ached with the awkward angle, twisting in my seat to face you square on. I ran my fingers through your hair. Our tongues wrestled and we both knew that we'd soon find the language of our bodies. Right now though, I don't know what to do with my hands. I don't want to ruin anything with unwanted advances. I kiss you, breathe, and stare at your face. *Not tonight,* you say. I pull back and breathe. I don't want to go yet, but the hours are rushing by and morning will bring work and reality. I need to sleep. I step out of the car and watch while you pull away. I should shower, but I won't. I don't want to wash away the smell of you on my skin. I want to remember the feel of your lips, your hands. I want to capture the night in my mind and save it there until I see you again.

The Girl Finally Arrives

I've been waiting for you since I was a kid. I don't know where you come from, but the summer is nearly here and the heat is starting to turn the mud to dust. The winds are blowing the smog out of the valley and the trees are turning new leaves toward the sun. Where have you been? I wish I knew your name. There's nothing going on here. Let's put on some music and dance for a while. Please stay, I didn't mean to frighten you. I just get excited when a face I've known my whole shows up and smiles at me. Can you stay the night? I'll sleep on the floor. You can have the bed. In the morning, we'll eat strawberries and joke about our families. I promise not to turn against you. I promise to be kind. I'll call you in a day or so and maybe, we can have drinks, but first I need to know, do you believe in love?

A Poverty of Touch

I wait for her to come out of the bathroom, naked and wet from the shower. I wait for her to notice me lying in bed, naked. She comes out and spares me a glance, just a glance, before dressing and leaving the room. Am I furniture, or a painting hung on the wall so long its familiar features are no longer noticeable? I wanted her to see me, but she didn't have time.

The night grows thick and dark as syrup poured from a glass jar. She sits in the living room typing. She has work to do. She has things on her mind.

I bring her a flower stolen from the neighbor's yard. *What's this?* She asks. *A token,* I say. *I'm not invisible.* She smells the flower and lays it next to her computer. *Love you,* she says. *Really?* She looks at me as if I'm a child. *Really,* she says. *I think of you all day.* It's nice to know, but it's hard believe. If she loves me, she would be able to see me. She'd be able to touch me with something like tenderness. It's been a month since she last reached out for me. Before the miscarriage, before the tragedy that's left us together, but unable to forgive the other.

Foreplay

The house is filled with the smell of yeast and rising dough.
You stand in the kitchen with flour dusting the apron you've
tied around your waist for this Sunday ritual. Your fingers
are thick and busy shaping the loaves. You roll out the
biscuits and slip them into the oven in time for supper. We'll
eat ham tonight and potatoes. Butter will melt and the
windows will fog with heat.

Outside, rain will fall and I'll stand in the courtyard
watching the sun finish its race through the sky. Somewhere
it's dawn and people are rising slowly from their beds to
wander into the day to do their work. I wait for the darkness
to fall and the rain to thicken before coming in and wrapping
my arms around your waist. Tonight we'll make love. Every
touch will be a promise.

I kiss the curve of your neck and taste the flour and salt
there. You rest your head on my shoulder and smell the
earthy smell of your hair. The kitchen will wait while we
explore the boundaries of foreplay. It's what I think about
through supper. It's what I think about washing the dishes
and counters. When everything is in its proper place, we
retreat to the bedroom and peel our clothes off in the yellow
light. We test the limits of flesh. We taste the salty taste of
sex. Afterwards, we shower and laugh. The night is still new,
but we lie in bed, flesh on flesh, whispering each other's
names.

No Beauty

Your scent is the first thing I notice in the morning. You smell of jasmine and sweat. I roll away from you for a moment and stand at the edge of the bed watching you sleep. Soon you will open your eyes and see me standing here, but right now, your face is smooth with sleep. The sun is just barely up and the birds are singing in the courtyard. The tree outside the bedroom window reaches into the sky, pulling the clouds to earth, blurring the lines of the world. You don't notice these things though. All you see is rain and you dress in a sweater and coat. Your hands grow cold and your feet wet. You walk out to the car and turn the heat up, waiting for the fog to clear from the windshield. You drive me to work and leave me there with a kiss.

When the day is done, you're there waiting for me and we go home where you stand on the patio and smoke a cigarette, shivering and muttering about the cold. You cannot see the beauty of the naked trees or the surprise of blue when a jay wings through the courtyard with a seed stuck in its bill.

We eat supper and sit in the living room watching the news. The world has grown dangerous and dark. People are dying and no one seems to notice the pattern of violence taking over the cities. When the sun goes down, we shower together and make love under the falling water. It's the first time all day you've been completely warm.

I cannot sleep yet, so I smoke and watch the cars on the street. The neighbors come home and move around their apartment, throwing fuzzy shadows on their curtains. I want to ask if they make love in the shower and go to bed early. I want ask if they know what it's like to lie in bed with someone who sees no beauty in the world.

More than a Rumor, Less than a Promise

We are more than just a passing rumor. She sits with me in the living room and smokes cigarettes, eating sardines from a paper plate. This is how it goes. We met at the library, talked about Heinlein and Robinson, and went for drinks afterwards. We met again over sandwiches at Tyson's down the street from my apartment. The first time she came over, she cleaned my kitchen and lectured me on tidiness. I thought I'd done well to vacuum my carpet. Now she sleeps in my bed and her face, dark and sweet, lies next to mine on the pillow. I kiss her eyelids and she smiles a secret smile. Her breath becomes mine and in the morning, I watch her rise naked and scuttle into the shower before she leaves for work. I don't know what she thinks about all day, but she comes home at night and touches my chest, reaching for my heart, making a glass of bourbon, and relaxing before making supper. When the sun drops into the mountains, we walk to the edge of town and wait for the moon to rise, silver in the velvet night. She is more than a fling, less than a marriage. We're caught somewhere in between, making do with what is and looking forward to what will be.

Lily

The floor rises up uneven and wobbly while I walk. She
holds me upright and leads me to the bed. I fall across the
mattress, unhinged and drunk. She pulls my clothes off,
piece by piece without saying a word. She folds the blankets
over me and I sleep with the spongy dreams boozes always
brings.

In the morning, she stands in the kitchen making eggs and
toast. I shower and wash away the smell of beer and whiskey
and cigarette smoke. I swallow four aspirin and eat in the
dining room. She stares at me and I finally ask her name.

Lily, she says and takes my empty plate. Sunlight crowds the
kitchen window and makes her hair stand out, golden and
thick. It never occurred to me that she was a stranger. I
remember her bringing me home.

I slept on the couch, she says. I feel bad now. I should've
offered her the bed, but I was too drunk to play the
gentleman.

I get my shoes and Lily washes the pans and plates from
breakfast. *Can I take you home?* I ask. She smiles. *I have a
car,* she says. I wonder why she stays, but it doesn't matter.
She's here now and I think I'm in love.

Travels

There is nothing I can do. I stand in the kitchen, the light
from the street pushing through the curtains. The sounds of
traffic soak the walls of my apartment. She brings her
dreams with her when she moves in. She wants a house
someday and children. I don't know what to tell her. She's
so young. My children are grown. I'll never make enough to
pay for a house. I can't reverse time and live my twenties
again. Maybe this is a bad idea, but she's here now and she's
begun to change the little things that make me comfortable.
I'll keep the silence for now. There's no point in picking a
fight, but soon she's going to realize that I'm an old man,
broken and wary of love. I should've thought through the
idea of living together. She's so young. Some day she'll
move on and fall for someone her own age. But right now,
she thinks I'm the answer to all of her questions. She doesn't
know that I'm just a pause in her travels from here to there.

Entanglement

Just the two of you, walking, be it on the street or in the park, the wooded hills at the end of town. He'll light a cigarette and the smoke will break in the wind, scattering. An eagle will fly from its nest and you'll revere its massive wings. Or maybe a dog will come to you and you'll stop for a second to rub its white coat. You'll walk and the walk will take you away from the home you've spent years building. When the sun sets, you'll return. You'll sit together in the living room, not talking, not looking at each other and when the time comes for sleep, you'll climb into bed, strangers who've known each other for years. It's strange to stand naked with him lying there with his eyes closed, with dreams already slipping through his mind like water through sand. He is not a bad man, but it's time to move on. In the morning, you tell yourself, I'll break the news. You'll pull yourself from this entanglement and sleep alone for a while, hoping to find love again.

A Lucky Man

A bottle of wine and roses in a vase. Candles on the table. A meal we'll share before bed. You are beautiful. Your face is long and narrow. I watch your hands cutting through the steak. You smile at me. *What're you looking at?* I look away, uncomfortable. I don't know what to say. Your face makes me warm; your hands comfort me. I can't help but stare. You're moonlight and rain. You're the spring wind promising summer heat. I am a lucky man, just sitting here with you, waiting for the night to close and the bed to cradle us while we make love.

Alone in the World

Living alone is an easy way to lose your mind. It's hard to
keep up with yourself. The floor is cluttered with takeout
boxes and the sink is full of dirty plates. The garbage smells
of bad food and the refrigerator is empty. You smoke in the
living room and write poems to pass the time. No one comes
here. No one knows that this is your world, not the street
outside, not the store at the end of the block. These little
rooms are all there is. They hold everything needing to be
held.

On Sunday, you do laundry, sitting in the plastic chair,
sleeping lightly while you wait for the dryer to finish its job.
You go home and drink beer while folding your clothes into
the drawers. Your voice is raw and unused. You haven't said
a word in days.

She knocks on your door and asks for an egg. *I'm making a
cake,* she says. You have no eggs and she goes back to her
apartment across the hall. You watch her walk away and
wish there was something you could do to make her stay.

Late in the morning, you sit on your balcony and watch the
people on the street. You want to say something, but you
don't know what. You would give anything to have a
conversation with an intelligent person. You'd love to have a
visitor, but you know no one and no one knows you.

After the Last Miscarriage

Bats hunt in the twilight sky. Clouds are gray and black as old ash. Tonight there will be no moon, no stars. The only light will come from living room windows and streetlamps. There will be rain and a miserable wind.

Soon it will be dark, you'll come home, and you'll lie on the couch with your eyes closed, frayed, and worn. I walk silently from room to room, careful of your nap. When you wake, we'll eat. You'll tell me about your day and I'll listen because that's what I do. I'll bring the baby up. You'll shake your head. *I can't get pregnant now,* you'll say. *I have too much to do.*

After your last miscarriage, you lost the drive. I can't blame you. I cried for hours myself, but I didn't have to lie there with legs in stirrup while a stranger scraped me out. I can only hope someday you'll get over it. I hope you'll heal.

Audry's Tongue

Audry burns for days with curiosity. Her neighbors haven't opened their curtains. They haven't come out to smoke their cigarettes. No one has said a word to her all week. She stares at their windows, willing someone to open one so she can ask where they've been, but the windows remain closed and she can't gather the latest gossip.

After a week, she calls the landlord and says she thinks something happened to the people living across the way from her. *They've left town for a while,* the landlords say. *Their rent is paid. There's nothing we can do.*

She goes back to her vigil. She smokes her cigarettes slowly and waits. No one comes. On Monday, she writes a note and slips it under their door. *Call me when you get back,* she writes. *I'm worried about you.*

On Wednesday, her neighbors drive up in their big diesel truck. They carry their suitcases up the stairs and she stands on her balcony waiting for them to come out to talk to her. She stands there for a long time, trying to look like she has a reason other than curiosity to be out in the weather.

Finally, the neighbor woman comes out and lights a cigarette. She notices Audry and smiles. *Thanks for the note,* she says. *It's nice to know there are people looking out for us.*

Where'd you go? Audry asks.

My father died. We went to Washington for the funeral.

Audry stops for a second. She doesn't want to push too hard. *I hope you had a good visit,* she says. The neighbor lady frowns. *It was a funeral,* she says. *No one had a good time.*

Audry blushes and turns away. She's missed her neighbors while they were gone, and now she wishes she'd kept her silence. But that's why she doesn't have many friends. Her tongue leads her to places best left alone.

A Young Woman Visits Her Mother

Miles pass and she thinks of the bridges back home. She thinks of the rain and the green trees, the lawns always growing. In the desert, rocks stand in the middle of wheat fields and orchards grow along the hillsides.

She stops at a gas station in a small town and fills her tank. She goes into the store, buys water, and pays for her gas. She drives away.

After the desert, there are mountains but they're not like the mountains back home. These mountains are round and aged, smooth from the wind. Juniper and Lodgepole Pines carpet their sides. She drives through the mountains and counts the clouds in the sky.

She arrives at her mother's house and stands in the lawn with the sprinkler on. She stands and stretches and her mother comes out to see her. It's only for a few days, but already she hears her mother complaining about the state of the world. Her mother blames her for being young. It's not something she can change. The problem can only be corrected with time.

A Temporary Patch

The angle of her face in the well-lit room makes a shadow on her chest. The nurses come and go. They bring her ice chips and painkillers. They check her cervix and pat her shoulder like this is a lunch date. Outside the window, the stars burn blue in the night. It's been four hours since her water broke. Pain makes her snappish and short. I keep my peace and hold her hand through the worst of it. I'm only a man, but I want to be here. I might not understand the nature of her pain, but I want to help. Talking doesn't help so I kneel by her side and wait for the baby to come.

The doctor arrives and catches the baby as she slides through the folds of her mother's flesh. I don't know what to do, so I watch the head come through, then the shoulders, belly, and legs. Blood and mucus make her slick. The nurses wrap her in a blanket and rush her to the warmer. She cries and it's the best sound in the world. They bring me to her side and I wash her with warm water and a soft cloth.

I bring her to her mother's breast and lay her there. She kicks and squirms in the blankets. Her mother smiles and laughs. This is what we've been waiting for. This is the reason we stayed together through everything. This child will bring us together for a short while, but she will not fix the broken heart.

What to Do with Herself

The pills make sleep come early and absolute. Night buries
the house in darkness. She lies in her bed thinking long,
wandering thoughts. Her neighbors move through the dim
light in the courtyard, talking about work. She listens for a
while, secretly thrilled to be eavesdropping.

When she sleeps, she sleeps without dreams. Hours pass
without notice. The stars do not bother her and the moon is
ignorant of the dangers of morning. When the sun rises, she
wakes and lies in her bed, warm and comfortable. She
doesn't want to move, but she cannot sleep anymore.

Coffee and toast fill her belly. She lights a cigarette, the
smoke rising in a thin cloud. She stands in the yard staring at
the wind. Jays flash blue in the shrubbery. Next door a dog
digs at the fence. If it gets out the whole neighborhood will
pay for its freedom.

She thinks she might move again this summer. She might
find a place in the country, away from the sounds of traffic
and neighbors who drink all night, playing their music in the
darkness. She thinks she might fall in love, but she doesn't
know when or how.

Men make her nervous and awkward. They make her weak
and quiet. They scare her. After her last lover left, she said
she'd live without their company. She'd be free of their
pushing ways. But it's been a year now and she doesn't
know what to do with herself.

When it's time to go to bed, she lies in the darkness counting
the taps on her window. There's a tree reach out to stroke the
glass. If she were braver, she'd cut the thing down. She's
burn the chunks in her iron stove, using all the love notes
she'd collected over the years.

132

Working on Work

Rain and a strong wind make the day dark, wet, and sad. She brings burgers home for dinner. We eat in the kitchen with paper plates. *What have you done today?* She asks. I bow my head. *Nothing,* I say. *I slept 'til noon. I watched the sun disappear behind a bank of clouds.*

She works hard and doesn't understand the lassitude of sadness. Things need doing and sitting all day in bed makes her crazy.

You have to do something, she says. *No one's going to rescue you from this.*

Tears wet my eyes. I don't want to be so sad all of the time. I want to be a woman who gets things done, but even the air is heavy on me. I cannot move.

Tomorrow, she says. *Tomorrow we'll find you a job.*

I nod and eat. I'll go to bed early tonight so I can look for work I won't be able to do.

What Age Brings Sometimes

A wind sings in the barn. A goat, old and worn nibbles the grass out front with a few chickens browsing for bugs. She walks through the big doors in front and up to the hayloft with its dust and piles of straw in the corners. She pulls out her lover's picture and stares at the face there, unreal and distant. This is where they first made love. This is the last place he'd come to find her. She just needs to be alone for a while before dinner and all the talk of work and chores. Their children are grown now and they're retired, looking for anything to fill the hours.

The dust here fills her sinuses and chokes her lungs. She won't stay long. They're delivering the corn to the food bank after they eat. It's something they do now. It gives them a chance to stop and talk to people they don't know.

After that, they'll come home and watch the television for an hour before going to bed. She'll rub his shoulders, but it'll go nowhere. Not since the prostate surgery. That part of their lives is over.

She puts the picture away and climbs down the ladder to the barnyard. She latches the gate behind her. Her lover is waiting in the kitchen with a roast chicken and pasta. They eat well, but it doesn't mean anything. She's lost her taste for food. She's lost her taste for anything that keeps the hours going. She won't do anything rash, but if a car crashed through the kitchen wall, she wouldn't step out of the way. At least then, it wouldn't be her fault.

Someday

We sit together on the patio smoking cigarettes, drinking
bourbon and water from short glasses. She reaches out to
touch my hand. An owl calls somewhere in the
neighborhood. The streets grow empty and silent.
Streetlamps make yellow light and the shadows are sharp
and dark. She says she loves me and I nod, not knowing
what to say. Of course I love her, but the words stick in my
throat like a shard of glass. My tongue is thick as the sole of
a shoe and my lips are numb. I nod and she waits. She asks if
I'll ever say the words. *Someday,* I say.

An Old Man's Day

Now is not the time for love. She's only been gone a year. I wear black to mark her death. I visit her grave every week. I cannot bring a woman into this.

She brings me coffee at the café and offers me breakfast, though I never eat. I drink my coffee and read the paper, looking for my wife's face in the pictures. It's never there, but I have to look.

I walk through town now and watch the cars on the street. All it would take is a simple miss-step and I'd be done. I'd go to my wife at last and we would be happy.

It's time to move on, my therapist says. *You need to find someone new.* But I'm not ready. My apartment is full of her photos. I can't take them down. They keep me safe.

On the bus, a woman sits next to me. She asks where I'm going. *Home,* I say. She nods. *Me too.* We sit silently for a while before she asks my name. *Isaac,* I say. She is Miranda.

The sun has fallen now. Streetlamps are hazy in the fog. I walk the last couple of blocks to my apartment and pour myself a glass of wine. I sit and stare at my wife's face on the wall.

Miss you, I say. *I want you back.* The silence is heavy here. The apartment grows dim with the night air. I finish my wine and go to bed. At least in my dreams I'm never alone.

William L. Alton

www.ingramcontent.com/pod-product-compliance
Lightning Source LLC
Chambersburg PA
CBHW020658260626
47157CB00008B/3081